MW00975894

From Here to There

Jae Henderson & Mario D. King

From Here to There

Printed in the United States

Put It In Writing
274 North Parkway
Memphis, TN 38105

This book is dedicated to anyone who ever dared to roll the dice of love and see where they landed. Remember that love is a beautiful thing, even when it's testing you to the fullest.

Foreword

What can we say? It's been a wonderful experience. This series grew out of a desire for two people to work together to better our black community by illustrating how we are weakening the structure of our families and therefor weakening the foundation of our communities. I think it's safe to say we did that. We wanted to illustrate black love and the beauty of it, and we did that. We wanted to show the importance of fighting to keep the black family intact, and we did that. Along the way we had the good fortune of meeting some new readers and making some new friends. We also learned more about the publishing processing and what it takes to be successful. As we end the Where Do We Go From Here series, we hope that you enjoyed taking this journey with us. Remember, our families are worth fighting for. Two individuals, raising their children together in love and harmony.

In addition to this series, we each have our individual projects and we hope you will continue to support us. Thank you for taking this journey with us.

Jae & Mario

Chapter 1

Natalie

"PUSH!! BREATHE! We're almost there!" said the doctor. My OBGYN, Dr. Sales, couldn't get here in time, so there's some man I have never met, all in my twat guiding me and my little one. He sounded like a drill sergeant as he forcefully instructed me on how to bring life into the world at a time when all I wanted to do was die.

I was in no shape to be delivering a baby, and the love of my life was in another part of the hospital fighting for his life. And now I'm here pushing and breathing for dear life without him. I didn't mean to upset Marcus. I just wanted to see my man, my baby daddy, the man I wanted to spend the rest of my life with. It didn't help that as they rolled me out, I saw Chanel standing outside the door. I wanted to roll that wheelchair right over her foot and kick her in the shin. I knew the only person that could have told her was Jackson; that man is so conniving. He had the nerve to offer to be in the delivery room with me. No way!

I silently prayed while I pushed. *Father God, please let Marcus be okay. Neither one of us has been perfect, but we are just starting to get it right. Have mercy on him. Have mercy on me.*

"You're doing just fine, Natalie . . . NOW, PUSH!!" the doctor instructed.

I bore down as hard as I could and gave a thrust to the lower half of my abdomen. I couldn't really feel the lower half of my body thanks to the epidural, but sweat was continuously rolling off the upper half.

"Now, one more big one should do it! PUUUUUUUUSH!" the doctor shouted.

I let out a sound that was a mixture of a grunt and a scream as I did as I was instructed. A few seconds later, he said, "Here—" then the doctor cut his sentence short.

I knew immediately that something was wrong, and I didn't hear any crying. There should be crying . . . Shouldn't there? I looked up at Mrs. Colbert. She hadn't said much. I knew she was mad at me for upsetting Marcus, but at least she was there. Even in her anger, she hadn't abandoned me in my time of need. She used her warm hands to give me reassuring touches the entire time, and now she gave me a forced smile as she wiped the sweat from my brow with a damp cloth. I opened my mouth to ask her what was wrong, but I suddenly felt tightness in my chest, as if someone had their fist wrapped around my heart. She looked in the direction of the doctor and stopped. Her stoic smile disappeared, and her face now held great concern.

"Code Blue. She's going into cardiac arrest!" I heard the doctor say.

"Stay with me, Natalie," said Mrs. Colbert. She said something else after that, but it was low and garbled. The kind, old woman was standing right next to me, but she sounded far away.

Out of nowhere came a blinding bright light. Then, in the glow appeared the glorious figure of a man. I couldn't quite recognize him, but the silhouette appeared to be that of . . . Marcus? It can't be.

Did I just die?

Is he dead?
Lord, help!

Chapter 2

Marcus

What good is it for someone to gain the whole world, yet forfeit their soul was one of the few verses I could remember from the Bible. My ignorance of other scriptures wasn't due to my disbelief, but rather, it was my reluctance to submit and become disciplined to the Word. Honestly, I wanted to dictate life on my own terms. My stubbornness, selfishness, and ego have always been the detriment to many of the relationships I endured throughout my life. Recently, I was fortunate enough to begin to understand the true meaning of family and relationships. And I was now able to begin to bear good fruit via my repaired roots and newly found peace from within. My ability to love unconditionally was renewed; I was happy, satisfied, and grateful for the opportunity at a second chance to make things right and to make my life right.

With life comes consequences. Much like life, the unpredictability of time doesn't always provide the possibility to right your wrongs or simply apologize. Apologize for the disappointments, hurt, and failures you've either caused or endured along the way. You may be asking why one would apologize if you're the receiver of the unfortunates. However, my answer would be that you're apologizing to God for not being able to forgive. That's how I'm feeling now. Just when I was at the apex of my manhood, it was all taken away from me. I was robbed of the opportunity to allow my maturity to flourish and hopefully enrich my new world with my son. If my dying was the price I had to pay to allow my son and Natalie a chance at a life full of peace, love, and fulfillment of purpose, then my life was a life well spent.

The "Good Book," as my dad always called it, is often referred to as the basic instructions before leaving earth, and one could never truly prepare to die. Just the thought of it had always provided me with an eerie feeling that shook the marrow within my bones. It just seemed so permanent—so final. Throughout my upbringing, the elders in my village would always say that death was the bridge to eternal life, but I never understood why one had to die only to live. My obsession was not with death itself, but the thought of it. I've always wondered what death would be like and how it would come upon me. As a child, I used to envision death as the guy in all black, creeping through my window carrying his scythe to prepare me for my final resting place. Death, to me, was like an incomplete sentence. There was so much more of my story to be told, only to end abruptly.

Now, as I stared into an empty space awaiting my fate, I began to reflect on my life and why it ended up this way. I always used to hear people say that your life will flash before your eyes before you die. I now understand fully what they meant. Visions from my days as a youth appeared like a cloud in the sky: playing pencil break with friends, eating Grandma's special rice pudding, my first loves, disappointments, and words I said were all played before me as if I were in my time of judgment. Empty tears began to trail the visions like rain as they became broken and began to drift, and a blinding light began to pierce through the darkness like the sun. No longer was my mind idle. It was now accompanied by the sound of life. With an accelerated beat of my heart, I opened my eyes, and I thanked God for the ability to love.

Chapter 3

Natalie

"Marcus, wake up! Baby, wake up!"

He was having that dream again. The one where he was in the holding room, that place where you go while your life hangs in the balance . . . purgatory. The way he explained it to me was that it's like God hasn't decided yet if you're going to live or die, so He puts you there while he makes a final decision. Perhaps He has made a decision, but he has decided to mess with your behind a bit more before he condemns you to the pit of hell. Who knows? I just know I never want to be there.

When I shook him, Marcus' eyes opened, and his face was covered in sweat. I grabbed a baby burping cloth off the nightstand, wiped his face, and kissed him gently on his moist forehead. He has been home for about a month now, and I hate to say it, but Marcus is a shell of the man he once was. He was in the hospital and a rehabilitation center for three months recuperating from that gunshot wound. It damaged the left side of his rib cage, took a small piece of his lung, and he lost a lot of blood. The doctors had to perform surgery to remove the bullet and repair his lung as best as they could. However, his recovery has been slow, but thankfully, it's been steady. He has to walk with a cane until he gains his strength back, but the doctor said he'll never make a full recovery.

He can probably get back to 80 percent and still live a good life. I don't think Marcus knows what a good life means right now. He's not in a very positive state of mind these days. Hell, I don't either. This is definitely *not* the life I imagined for the three of us.

I've had my own share of challenges. I had a mild heart attack after I gave birth, but I'm okay. Our little trooper, Trenton, is fine too. Although he had some problems breathing when he was first born, and he had to stay in the NICU for a couple of weeks, but he's fine now. Thank God. According to the hospital staff, that was the first time they had to treat a mother, father, and child simultaneously, and they weren't all involved in a car accident. That's a moment in black history that I wish the three of us could have avoided.

The good thing is we're not alone. My grammy is back! She came down from Detroit to help, and she has been a godsend. Caring for Marcus, Trenton, and me would have been too much by myself. Also, I recently went back to work. One of us had to. I wasn't going to sit here and watch both of us deplete our savings and 401(k)s when I was fully capable of working, and Jackson was true to his word and helped me find another job. Good old faithful, conniving Jackson. It's obvious that Marcus misses his boy, but he did the unforgivable. He tried to get with his baby's momma. Although Jackson and I are cool, we came to an understanding that we can't be best friends and hang out like we used to, but we don't have to be enemies. With his recommendation, I landed a job at Powell, Johnson, and Haynes as a junior management trainee. It's quite a step up from reception-ist. I'm in the process of finishing my producer's license so that I can make some major coins to take care of my family until my man gets back to his old self—*if* he ever gets back to his old self.

Marcus lay there for a few minutes with his eyes open, staring at the ceiling, and I rose from the bed to get him some water. When I returned, he was sitting up with this strange look on his face.

"Good morning, Handsome," I said as I kissed him on the cheek and handed him the water. He didn't respond but gulped it down. While he quenched his thirst, I headed to the bathroom and got a cool towel to wipe his face. He was still sweating. I peered over into Trenton's crib; his rosy cheeks looked almost cherubic. He let out a small sigh, stretched, and continued his sleep in his Mickey Mouse onesie. Since Grammy was in his room, he was sleeping in the room with us, and I like it that way so that I can keep a close eye on both my boys.

When I got back to Marcus, he traded me his now-empty cup for the towel and wiped the sweat from his drenched brow.

"I'll be glad when these dreams stop," he said. He had that sexy, early-morning raspiness in his voice. It's always been a major turn-on for me. Trenton interrupted my soon-to-be lustful thoughts with a loud wail. I hate hearing my baby cry. He's probably hungry, which was one of the first lessons I learned as a new mother; newborns are *always* hungry. I moved to his crib and picked him up.

I love this little guy so much. He opened his eyes and let out another loud wail. I know how to shut him up. I pulled up the I'm A Good Woman shirt I slept in last night and put him in his favorite position, the one where he gets to drink his fill of his mommy's delicious milk. He immediately stopped crying and began suckling as if his life depended on it.

I don't particularly enjoy breastfeeding, because it's uncomfortable and even painful at times, but I do it because all the books I have read stated that mother's milk is the best thing for babies. My once-large breasts are now huge and heavy, especially when he hasn't eaten, or I haven't pumped. I felt Marcus watching me. I winced. I have to remember to get some of that nipple butter I heard about to help with chaffing.

"Do you have to go to work today?" he asked.

"Yes, we're trying to retain a corporate client with 15,000 employees, and if we can offer them our best insurance benefits package, it will be a major boost for the company. The presentation is in a few weeks, and I am on the research team," I replied.

He let out a loud sigh. "This condo is lonely without you."

I chuckled. "You mean you don't have anyone to wait on you hand and foot."

Grammy assists, but she said she's not anyone's maid, and she believes that Marcus should start doing the things he can do for himself.

After a long thought, I said to him, "Then why don't you go out. It's supposed to be nice outside today. Don't you have physical therapy?"

"No. It's tomorrow."

I heard a soft knock on the door. "Come in," I said.

It was Grammy. She still had her stocking cap on, with her large pink sponge rollers on her head, which always made me laugh. With all the inventions for women to protect their hair while they sleep, scarves, do-rags, bonnets, and more, she still chooses to cut off a pair of old pantyhose and wear them on her head.

"Good morning, you two," she said.

We both responded, "Good morning, Grammy," in unison.

"What would the adults like to eat this morning? I see the little one is already having his breakfast."

I looked at Marcus. He shrugged.

"It doesn't matter. Surprise us. I'm not very hungry," he said softly.

I smiled at her. This woman would move a mountain for me if I needed her to, and I would do the same for her. "Well, I'm starving. Can I have some of your world-famous cheese grits?"

She hadn't put her teeth in yet and gave me a gummy grin. Grammy loves when people compliment her cooking.

"Of course, you can, baby. Give me thirty minutes."

"Thanks, Grammy." She flashed those gums at me again and quietly closed the door as she exited the room.

"How long is she going to be here? I appreciate her help, but I would like to feel like I'm home. I can't walk around in my underwear or scratch my nuts while I watch ESPN with her here," said Marcus.

I paused and stared at him before answering. Was he serious? "As long as she needs to be. I'm a new mother and a working one at that. We could use the help."

"I'll hire someone who has to go home every day."

"We can't afford that right now, Marcus. Between the three of us, we have a ton of medical bills, and may I remind you that you have another child on the way, which will be another bill."

It felt weird having to tell Mr. Deep Pockets to be concerned about money. When we met, he was making six figures and had no kid responsibilities, which meant plenty of discretionary income. He is currently on a long-term leave of absence from his job. They told him that whenever he is ready to come back to his old position, it would be waiting for him. He has short-term disability coverage through his insurance, but that will end in a few months. Without knowing how long it would take him to recuperate, I wanted to be mindful of how we spend our money. On the other side, Marcus' condo and two vehicles come with a hefty monthly fee. He can't drive either right now, but we still have to pay the notes and insurance, and not to mention the mortgage. At some point, I plan on talking to him about selling one car and trading the other in for something cheaper but not right now. He was having a hard enough time dealing with his weakened physical state.

I usually look forward to going to work; it's my escape from everything that's wrong with my relationship. I used to be so crazy about Marcus. I love him, but I'm not so sure I'm still in love with him. Many of the things I loved about him were stripped away. His self-confidence is low, and we don't talk or joke like we used to. We don't even make love anymore because he always says he's not in the mood. He even turns down head! What man in his right mind turns down oral sex? I asked him what was wrong, but he wouldn't tell me. I think he's afraid that he won't perform like he used to. He's probably right. With a piece of his lung missing, he gets winded easily, and I'm trying to be understanding, but I have needs that are being ignored. I was optimistic that he would return to his old self in time, but the question is, how long? We have a kid, and Marcus was my sunshine on a cloudy day. He always had a way of making me smile, even when I didn't want to. His "can-do" attitude was refreshing, and his sex was energizing. Now, both are absent when I need them the most. This new position is scary and the most responsibility I've ever had. As a secretary, if I messed up the correspondence on a letter, no big deal, but if I mess up the insurance benefits of an entire company or botch the proposal, and we don't get the contract, it's a *huge* deal. My entire career is riding on getting it right.

I have to leave the house today for another reason besides work, though. I recently got a text from his other baby momma, Chanel. That bald-headed wench said she needed to talk to me. About what, I don't know. I guess she had to contact me. When Marcus was in the hospital, I got him a new phone with a new number. I needed him to leave all those women in his past in his past. He is with me now and only me. He is in no position to help Chanel, anyway. I know she keeps in touch with Marcus' mother, and that has been the way she gets her updates. Mrs. Colbert and I both let it be known that she was not a welcomed visitor when Marcus was in the hospital, but she could call either of us if she needed something while he was there. I guess she preferred to talk to Mrs. Colbert instead of me.

Trenton finished draining my left breast and started to whimper while I shifted him to my right.

The funny thing is that since Marcus has been out of the hospital, he hasn't asked about Chanel or their baby. I mention them from time to time just to get him to say something. But he told me that he wanted to focus on the family he has at hand right now. He will worry about them when she gets further along, and I feel sorry for her. I couldn't imagine going through my pregnancy without Marcus. He was there the entire time, but that's what she gets for trying to come between my man and me. He has always been mine, and I just needed him to realize it. Chanel should be about four or five months along. I wonder what she's having.

I hope it's not a boy. Hell, she was the reason I named our son Marcus. I was afraid that she would try to give Marcus a namesake to make sure he was taken care of if Marcus took a turn for the worst. If anyone is going to be named Marcus, it's going to be *my* son. So, I named him Marcus Trenton, and I made sure she got the news that I did.

Chanel said it was important, and she had no desire to talk about it over the phone. I agreed to meet her for lunch. She had better not try to start any shit. I'm a nursing, hormonal mother with a recuperating man, and I don't have time to play with anyone.

Chapter 4

Marcus

I let out a long and agonizing sigh as I stared blankly at another exasperating television show that Natalie loved to watch. I'm not one to judge or complain. I used to be but not now. But I admit that it's been human torture to have to sit through episode after episode of meaningless, drama-filled reality shows. Yet, if that's the escape she needs from our current state of reality, then I will continue to participate in the grueling event.

When I heard the front door close, I lay down again in an attempt to ease the excruciating migraine that is annoying me like an infectious itch. I closed my eyes briefly, only to be interrupted by the wail of a child that was in no mood to go back to sleep. With slight pain and pressure on my right side, I eased back up.

"Hey, little fella, what's all the grumpiness about? Are you missing Momma already? Me too, little one, me too," I said. Uncomfortably, I reached for my little guy who was wrapped snuggly lying atop the pillow cushion my mother bought for him. "You don't like watching this shit on television either, do you?" I asked as I reached for the remote control that was mysteriously hiding behind Natalie's pillow. As I changed the station to something a little more upbeat and intellectually stimulating, Natalie's Grammy opened the door.

There she stood with those tight-ass pantyhose on her head and thin nightwear that exposed her extra-large, supersized drooping breasts. I'll have to talk to Natalie about getting her a robe. We should call her Big Momma instead of Grammy.

"You want me to take that little cupcake out of here so you can get up and get out?"

I wasn't particularly fond of Grammy being here, but I was thankful. She's been more than cordial and a tremendous amount of help. Despite our rather rough beginnings, we are all right now.

"We're fine, Grammy," I said. "This little guy just wants a little attention from his ol' dad." Still standing in the doorway, she placed her hand on her hip and adjusted what looked to be a girdle underneath her nightgown, and replied, "Fine by me, but yesterday was the last day you gonna sit around here and loaf around in that bed. All asses must be out of the bed and out and about from here on out. You got one hour to do so."

Feeling a little perplexed about her position, I blurted out, "Grammy, I was shot. I should be on bed rest!"

She returned a look that I have begun to know all too well. It's her "you about to get a piece of my mind" look. After about three pats to the top of her head in an attempt to ease the itch that was happening underneath them tight-ass pantyhose on her head—which quite possibly could be causing the itch—she replied, "Is you alive?"

Still looking a little dumbfounded, I replied, "Uh, yes. I hope so."

"Well, if you're alive, then you need to do as such and be alive. We all know you was shot or whatnot, but what you can't and ain't gonna do is think you're about to lie around here and cry over spilled milk. Did you get shot? Yes. Did you die? No. So, get your ass up."

I didn't even get a chance to get the last word in b cause she closed that opportunity by shutting the door. All I heard was her singing an off-key made-up song at the top of her lungs, *"You gots one hour to get, get, get, get your ass out the beeed,"* as her voice faded to oblivion. I looked at my little fella who looked as if he had a slight grin on his face. "Your Gram-Gram is crazy as hell," I said as I looked into his eyes. *I guess I better get, get, get—get my ass out the beeed*, I sang to his amusement.

Being a man who has been in control and used to being a mover and shaker the majority of his adulthood, my current state has been a struggle, to say the least. Natalie has been frustrated as of late, and this new life is an adjustment for both of us. Don't get me wrong, we share laughs here and there, but there is still some level of unknown tension or distance that exists between us. My mind often drifts to different possibilities, as it could be a number of things: Chanel and the baby situation, me not being in working condition, monetarily or sexually, and then there are still the lingering effects from that night. My nightmares are constant, and I don't like opening doors. I panic at the sound of doorbells or sudden knocks. My night sweats are not the sexiest scene, and let's be honest, I've been a complete bore as of late.

Applying as much pressure as I can on my cane, I rose to my feet. Staring directly at me no more than three feet was my reflection. I thought to myself, *Grammy is right. I'm alive, and I should act as such.* Staring at the man in the mirror with his unkempt hair and disheveled beard, he no longer resembled the man he used to be. Snapping out of my slight trance, I noticed that Trenton was now starting to doze off again. Struggling less with each step,

I mustered up as much strength as I could and placed him gently into his crib. Out of all the things that had gone wrong of late, Trenton is the one thing that I have been able to get right. I was indeed blessed to have both Trenton and Natalie in my life, especially in my time of need.

I limped my way to the bathroom to take a shower. Taking a shower was a pleasure for me because it seemed to ease my pain and made a great place to think. A multitude of thoughts flashed through my mind as the hot water ran down my weakened body. However, for some reason, my thoughts always seemed to drift back to my exes Chanel and Lisa and my current, Natalie. I was relieved that Lisa and I had a chance to speak after the accident. We needed the closure that both of us deserved, even if it was unpleasant. As for Chanel, I did have a lot of love for her, but our timing and situations were too much for us to handle. In a perfect world, meaning if she wasn't a part of Lisa's and my past, maybe things would have worked out differently. After all, she was my perfect imperfection. Chanel and I still had our situation to handle as well. In our last conversation prior to my being shot, we had what I perceived to be an understanding, but I'm not too sure if that is still the case. Natalie and I are still a work in progress, and I've grown to understand and love her more as each moment passes. Life and its complexities are the master Chinese puzzle.

When I emerged from the shower, I found that Grammy had been there. She had stolen little Trenton away from me, ironed, and laid out the clothes she picked for me to wear. I actually liked what she put together. I swear that little old woman can be mean at times, but she has the heart of an angel. I laid out some accessories to go with it: my Movado watch, platinum bracelet, and my favorite necklace, a crucifix Natalie bought for me. If I was going out, I was going out in true Marcus Colbert style. I was interrupted by the sound of the phone Natalie purchased for me not too long ago, so I rerouted my direction toward the phone.

"This is Marcus." Even though I've been out of the business world for a few of months, I still answered the phone like a professional.

"Hey, big brother. How is everything going?"

"Hey, you. I'm not doing the best, but I'm alive, right?"

"That's good to hear. Listen, I was thinking about coming over this weekend and spending some time with you and my nephew. Is that cool?"

I must admit that it was good hearing from my little sister. Ever since the incident, Mia had been very distant. She didn't handle it very well, and she'd been going to counseling about it. "Of course. I think that would be great." There were some other things I needed to discuss with her as well. Natalie shared with me some of the activities she had been up to over the last couple of months, and I needed to find the underlying cause of some things. For those very reasons, I refuse to let her keep one of my cars, even though she has asked several times. So maybe this visit would be a little therapy for both of us.

"Great. I'll get Momma to drop me off."

After I said my goodbyes, I journeyed to the bathroom and tried to ease myself into my old routines, to no avail. My mind wanted me to do things that my body just couldn't or wouldn't do with ease. I was beyond frustrated because everything took so long, and then there was the pain: Brushing my teeth was a struggle, stepping into the shower was hell, and God forbid I had to put on lotion—that was the worst! I endured pain in parts of my body that I didn't even know existed.

Amid my discomfort, I reached for my deodorant that was wedged between Natalie's jewelry box and an assortment of items I couldn't name if I tried. As I picked up the deodorant, a tiny piece of folded paper fell from the inside corner of the jewelry box. Normally, I would have ignored it, but my anxiety had gotten the best of me. Feeling like a top-secret spy, I began to peel back the layers of this mystery and unfolded the paper, corner by corner. My eyes widened, beads of sweat began to build atop my forehead, and my heart accelerated. My migraine returned. I leaned forward to prevent myself from tumbling to the ground as I reached for the nearest bottle of painkillers that were on the other end of the dresser. I angrily swallowed two pills. Confusion had set in, and the anger and hurt continued to build. I looked back at the letter that had been written by Jackson and just crumbled as a man. A man who had been broken.

Chapter 5

Natalie

I was enjoying my new job. I loved the salary. The benefits were more than adequate, and the people were pleasant. It was an environment where people wanted you to succeed, and you could tell. I was always receiving advice and encouragement from my superiors, who obviously believed in me and what I could bring to the company. Several of the trainees, like me, shared an assistant, and her name was Shari. Shari was tall and skinny and a little younger than I, but she had a nurturing spirit that surpassed her years on this earth. She also had the smoothest bronze skin I had ever seen. It seemed to shimmer. She once told me that she was biracial. Her mother was Italian and a former model, and her father was a tall, dark-skinned Dominican. She was dating some rich, white man she met while getting coffee for the office a few months ago. He called her his "mocha goddess." Shari was always nicely dressed, and she spoke with a very mild accent. Some of her comments and actions made me think that she was bisexual, but I decided not to ask—some things I didn't want to know.

"Good morning, Ms. Tellis," she said as I approached her desk. She got up and helped me out of my coat.

"Good morning, Shari. I keep telling you that you don't have to do this. I can take my own coat off. You can also call me Natalie. How was your weekend?"

"I don't mind. I get to take a whiff of that wonderful perfume you wear. What are we wearing today, *Ms. Natalie*?" She moved her face closer to my neck and breathed in.

I laughed and took a step back. I guess being formal and invading my personal space was a part of her nature. "Kisses by Rihanna. I never thought I would love her fragrances the way I do, but they are heavenly. I plan to try her makeup line next."

Shari then eyed me up and down and gave me a thumbs-up to signify that she approved of my outfit. Today, I wore a pair of winter-white wool slacks and a matching mohair sweater. I upgraded my wardrobe with a little help from Jackson when I landed the job. Marcus would kill me if he knew I still accepted money from him, but I wanted to make a good impression, and it seemed I had.

"I agree. She is truly one talented sista. My weekend was wonderful. I went with my boyfriend to his parents' lake house. It was so relaxing. There's something about nature that just calms every inch of you. Would you like coffee or tea this morning? How was your weekend?"

Shari is truly a sweetheart. She always seemed genuinely concerned about me and my needs. "I'm in a tea kind of mood. I'm glad you had the chance to get away. Mine was the usual, attending to my infant child and my ailing boyfriend."

"How's he doing?"

"He's progressing. It's going to be awhile before he gets back to his old self, but in time, he'll be fine. I'm just glad he's still here with us. Thanks for asking. Can you bring me the Waterhouse Publishing file?

"Will do, Ms. Tellis. I mean Natalie. It's so nice to have you here. There aren't too many of us people of color at the company, and before you came, the ones who are here act like them. They think they have to assimilate into white society to succeed. You keep it real and don't apologize for being you," said Shari.

"I appreciate the compliment, honey. I was raised to be proud of who I am and where I come from. This company said they wanted diversity, and that doesn't mean hiring clones of what they already have. I appreciate you looking out for me the way you do."

I gave Shari a quick hug and headed to the office I share with two other trainees. Our desks were strategically placed around the room to give each of us our space but no privacy. I think they did it that way on purpose so that we can spy on each other and keep our competitive edge.

I try not to engage in too much banter in the morning. I need to get straight to work. I needed my supervisors to see that I'm productive on company time. Shari brought the tea and the file I asked for, and I put my DO NOT DISTURB sign on my desk. I started using the sign when I realized that no one seemed to care if I looked preoccupied and would stop by my desk at any given time to chat. To be at my best, I need to focus. Therefore, to remedy that problem, I created that sign and let it be known that if that sign is up, I would appreciate it if others would just speak and keep it moving . . . or better yet, not speak. Mindless friendly banter was not wanted nor appreciated. We could talk at lunch, and most people respected it.

I am determined to outshine all the other trainees and hopefully end up with my own office with a door I can close to thwart distractions. It's my job to review what benefits package Waterhouse Publishing was currently offering its employees to see how we could enhance it. It was almost time to renew their contract, and several of our competitors were trying to woo the seventy-five-year-old publishing giant away from us, and I wasn't having it. I was going to sweeten that package and put a cherry with whipped cream on top while turning a nice profit for the company.

About four hours later, it was almost time for me to meet with Chanel, and I arranged to take a two-hour lunch so I could swing home and check on Marcus and Trenton. I know Grammy is there, but seeing my adorable son in the middle of the day seemed to make the rest of the day just fly by. I wasn't really looking forward to seeing Chanel, but I was more than a little curious about what the bald homewrecker had to say.

I took a deep breath, gathered my things, and headed out of the building. I arrived at Bricktops Restaurant looking like I ran the damn world. I made sure that every inch of me screamed bougie, blessed, and unbothered. She may be having Marcus's baby too, but I had Marcus. Even in his broken state, he was still a hell of a catch.

Chanel had already arrived, and the hostess escorted me to where she was sitting. As I approached the table, I noticed that my arch nemesis didn't look so hot. Her short afro looked like it hadn't been moisturized or combed in a couple of days. She didn't have on any makeup, and she looked sleep-deprived as well with deep bags under her eyes. Maybe pregnancy wasn't agreeing with her. Some women are a ball of energy, while others seem completely void of it. My experience was somewhere in the middle until all those false deliveries. It was obvious that Chanel had put on a few pounds, but I attributed that to the baby weight.

I gave a curt hello and sat down without taking off my coat because I didn't intend to stay long. She smiled, "You look great. How are you?"

"I'm fantastic. New baby, great man; life couldn't be better. And yourself? You look tired."

Her smile disappeared. "I am. Well, why don't I get straight to the point since being cordial doesn't seem to be your strength. I asked you here to tell you, you won."

"I won? What do you mean? This isn't a competition."

She scratched her unkempt head and scoffed. I bet that there's a ton of dirt and dandruff up there.

"Oh, isn't it? We were pitted against each other from the very beginning, vying for the same man's affections. We were both hoping to build a life with Marcus, and then we both conceived his child. Don't you see how we were both manipulated? He gave us both false hope and good sex," she said.

The waitress approached our table, and I placed my drink order. Chanel was already sipping a hot tea. I sat quietly until the waitress left. As I stared at Chanel's face, I could see the anger and hurt in her eyes. Marcus was wrong, but we are both grown women, and we each have to accept our role in this.

"Chanel, I know this isn't an ideal situation for you, but Marcus told you that he had a baby on the way with another woman early in your courtship, and you chose to pursue a relationship with him anyway."

"That's where you are wrong. Marcus knew he had a baby on the way with another woman, and he *chose* to pursue me. A man with honor and integrity would have focused on the woman and child he had at hand instead of bringing another person into his mess. He also would have taken precautions not to get me pregnant," she said.

"Whoa, Mother Teresa. You dated him of your own accord. *My man* didn't whop you over the head, say come with me, and open your legs. You got exactly what you wanted, your best friend's ex-boyfriend that you always coveted. You've had your eye on Marcus for years, and you couldn't pass up the chance to have him no matter what the cost. You just didn't bank on a baby momma being part of the deal."

Chanel rolled her eyes, started digging in her large Louis Vuitton purse, and pulled out a pack of cigarettes.

Was she serious? "This is a nonsmoking restaurant, and you shouldn't be smoking in your condition," I said and tried to snatch them away.

She moved. "Don't touch me. What condition is that? Depressed and alone? These calm my nerves."

I rolled my eyes. "Look, Marcus never meant to abandon you. He was shot, and in his current state, he's not much good to anyone. He's taking it day by day. He plans to be a good father to both of his children."

"Why are you defending him? He could at least call. I don't even have his number. I can't come to see him because you and your grandmother are at his house, and I don't feel like the drama."

I gritted my teeth and said, "First, that is *our* house. He lives there with *his family*, and you are damn right . . . you aren't welcome! As for the calls, I don't think he quite knows what to say. His recovery is going slowly, and it's been hell for his self-esteem. He's not the same Marcus."

Chanel laughed. "He's not the same? Well, I've changed too, and I'm no longer his concern. I lost the baby." She dug deeper in her purse and pulled out a lighter, extracted a cigarette from the pack, and lit it. I didn't try to stop her. As the tip burned, she took a long drag and blew it out.

I sat dumbfounded by that magnificent news. Christmas came early. I wasn't even going to pretend to feel bad for her or to possess eympathy for her situation. She was about to leave our lives forever.

She must have noticed my joy. "It's okay. I don't expect you to care. I lost our child about two weeks ago. I decided to tell you so that you could tell him because I don't want to hear from Marcus Colbert ever again as long as I live. He ruined my life."

The waitress returned with the water with lemon I requested. I took a large gulp, then said, "There you go blaming him again for your unwise decision-making," I said.

"You're damn right. I didn't ask him to ask me out. I didn't ask him to make me feel better than any man ever has before. I didn't ask him to make me his woman. I didn't ask to fall in love and conceive his child. And I damn sure didn't ask him to abandon me for his other baby mother, get shot, and forget we exist. It's like everything he and I had was a lie. I see now I was just a way for him to get over Lisa and escape you."

What did this bitch say? "What? Escape me?"

She smirked. "Of course. You should have heard the way he talked about how you were a basic broad, and the best thing about you was sex. He talked about how he was going to have to be the one to make sure that your child was well-rounded and exposed to the finer things in life and culture because all you did was watch reality TV and dress up your stupid dog. He said you had no aspirations in life and regretted sleeping with you. He went on and on about how he got caught slipping in a major way, and he knew your basic ass thought you were on the come-up because you landed a big-time corporate executive like him. According to him, all he wanted to do was get through your pregnancy and take care of his child. You and I both know he wasn't over Lisa. He never loved either of us. I hear he slept with her while in Seattle on a business trip. Is that true?" She then took a sip of her tea and smirked again.

I was not going to address her question. Marcus and I had already worked through his infidelity and his untimely relationship with Chanel. Our focus was on our family and his health. "I don't believe you. Marcus loves me. And, yes, he might not have thought much of me at first, but once you were out of the picture, and he really got to know me, he realized that there is much more to me than meets the eye. You can't hurt me because, remember, as you said, *I won*."

Chanel took another drag of her cigarette and let it out. "Girl, please. You were the consolation prize. He couldn't have Lisa. I told him to kick rocks after I found you trying to suck his dick. That was such a desperate attempt to get him back with the only skills you have. Of course, he chose you. He had no place to go, and the child support payments you were planning to stick him with would have crippled his income. Now he's sick and needs someone to take care of him, and there you are, his basic baby momma-turned-nurse and breadwinner. Yep, you won, but it doesn't look like much of a prize if you ask me."

My blood was boiling, and I wanted to take that hot tea and throw it right in her face. I struggled to keep my composure while I said, "You don't know shit about me."

Chanel took another long drag on her cigarette and released the smoke. "You're right. I don't, but Marcus does, and he was none too pleased with what he'd learned over the past year while he was dicking you down. So enjoy your baby and your disabled man, *bitch*." She took another long drag on her cigarette, and this time, she blew the smoke in my face.

I started coughing. I hate smoke. I was about to reach across the table and slap her, but unexpectedly, a laugh grew from the bottom of my belly and worked its way up. I was certain I could whoop her behind, but there was no need. She was already down for the count and looking for someone to blame. She hadn't realized that she didn't need to look any further than her mirror. Chanel was so pathetic.

Chanel didn't get the angry reaction she expected. "What's so funny?" she asked with a perturbed expression.

"You. You are bitter, Chanel, and it's so thick within you, it's seeping out of your pores. What's wrong? Is the preacher's daughter tainted? I know how your situation has spread through your daddy's megachurch like wildfire. Nationally renowned pastor's baby girl got herself knocked up by another woman's man. Tsk-tsk. She now wears the scarlet letter on her forehead, H for harlot, maybe it's F for fornicator, perhaps it's P for pathetic, or maybe it stands for played. You're no longer daddy's prized possession. He was so proud of you. I heard how he would tell other single women that they should be like you—a strong woman of God full of virtue waiting on the Father to send her Boaz. It's so much easier to blame Marcus than to admit you got weak and gave in to temptation because you were getting desperate. You're about to be thirty-five, aren't you, and not a viable candidate in sight. You thought you could just waltz in and get Marcus once Lisa left, but you didn't count on the fact that I was going to fight for mine, or that he actually had feelings for me. With all your degrees and Black Power prowess, you lost the man of your dreams to a mere receptionist, and you can't stand it. I'm a lot smarter than you think, and I deserve everything that comes my way—the baby, the man, and all his undying devotion and love. I won't allow you to tear me down to build yourself up. Honey, I'm living the good life."

Chanel angrily stubbed her cigarette out on the saucer in front of her that once held the cup that contained her tea. "I hope you both get everything you deserve, and it ain't happily ever after. God doesn't bless mess. The very foundation of your relationship is cracked. You were a friendship with benefits. If you hadn't gotten pregnant, he wouldn't be with you, and you know it. You were nothing more than convenient and all too willing pussy. At least I was his girlfriend when I got pregnant. Can you say the same? You've had his baby, and he hasn't even offered you a ring, just cohabitation in his house. I don't know why I thought I could talk to you woman to woman. We're both the victims of a manipulative man who thinks with his penis, but you're too dumb to see it. He's already cheated on you once. Do you honestly think that he won't do it again once he's recuperated?"

I wasn't 100 percent the answer was no, but I wasn't going to let Chanel know that. She needed to worry about herself. "Read your Bible more. God has taken many a mess and made it a masterpiece. Marcus has changed," I said. "But you wouldn't know that because you haven't seen or talked to him in months. He went to all my doctor appointments. He talked to my stomach and sang our baby songs. He rubbed my feet and massaged my shoulders. He made love to me with his magnificent mouth when I was too pregnant to do anything but lie there. Did you get any of those things? Nope! He didn't have to get back with me. He wanted to. Your reality is twisted sister, and so are you."

"Fuck you and him!" she screamed. "I see losing this baby was the best thing that could have happened to me because I am free of this drama." Chanel then scooted out of the booth we shared and headed to the door as fast as her feet would carry her. There weren't many patrons in the restaurant, but now those few were staring my way trying to see what the commotion was about.

"Goodbye and good riddance!" I yelled after her. I sat there for a few minutes and drank my water to compose myself. Slowly, everyone went back to what they were doing before our spat interrupted their lunch. The things Chanel said truly bothered me. Marcus was downing me to another woman while I was carrying his child. That was low. He was building her up while tearing me down. Was he really with me because he had no one else and he needed someone to take care of him? I changed my mind about going home. Marcus Colbert was the last person I wanted to see at that moment.

Chapter 6

Marcus

Commitment was an ideal that continued to sit over my head like an overbearing weight. Commitment to life. Commitment to peace. Commitment to love. Commitment to forgive. These commitments were nothing more than pieces to the puzzle to complete my recovery. I was honest in my intentions. Pure. Faithful. Open. I must admit that the latter commitment to forgive was something that would ultimately be the toughest hurdle for me to climb over.

Getting out of the house was a huge step for me on my road to recovery. When I speak of recovery, I'm not referring to a relapse to the man I was; I'm more so referring to a leap to become the man I want to be. After the recent altercation that led me to getting shot in the chest—thank God it wasn't my head—I've been having bad dreams that were reminders of the day I was beat up by Natalie's brother and their friend, Manny, while jogging in the park. I haven't told Natalie that some of my nightly sweats were because of that incident. I, for one, would love to move on from that, and I'm sure she believes that I have. Honestly, I thought I did. Subconsciously, my mind has been preventing my heart from being able to let it go. I've been mentally digging up the paranoia dirt that had been buried beneath the mounds of newfound happiness and joy. I guess that was why I had such a negative reaction when I found that letter that was penned by Jackson.

Never did it cross my mind that Jackson would be the one who pulled the trigger. Did we have our differences? Yes, but that didn't mean that he would have the heart to do such a thing. But did he have a heart? Hate and a vengeful mind can cause the heart to do irregular things one might not have control over. Jackson was in that space. I couldn't quite understand why Natalie would continue to entertain the thought of having a friendship with a person who very well could be the one who orchestrated the shot that almost ended my life. However, there isn't any evidence indicating such, and he has a strong alibi that has kept him clear of any guilt or association to the crime. At the time it occurred, he was in the ER after having an allergic reaction to a dish he tried at a new restaurant.

As I sat on the bench, I leaned my head toward the sky, closed my eyes, took in the crisp midafternoon air, and allowed it to ease my mind. I needed something to uncloud my judgment. I no longer wanted my insecurities or anger to be the catalyst for my actions that were to come. With an open mind and expanded sense of my surroundings, I just listened. First, it was the sound of the birds chirping that were gliding to and from the barren apple tree to my left. Next was the sound of laughter escaping the lips of the little ones enjoying one of the greatest pleasantries of life—innocence. I then keened in on the sound of the wind intimately moving and swaying. Finally, I was able to lock in and listen to my own thoughts and inner being. I was able to listen to the pace of my heart decrease. I was able to listen to the calmness that alleviated my migraine. I was able to hear peace. That is a sound I hadn't been able to hear for quite some time. For when one finds peace, he can forgive.

When I opened my eyes, I knew the next thing I needed to do was make that phone call. It was a phone call that I dreaded with each thought, but it was a call that was necessary.

Jackson answered on the first ring. "I never expected to hear your voice again. Despite all that we've been through, I must say that you've been on my mind." He sounded happy, almost elated. I couldn't say the same.

I allowed for some empty space to cause a little discomfort within the conversation. I wanted it to feel awkward. After all, this relationship wasn't comfortable, and it was awkward, to say the least, so I treated it as such.

"I will be honest and state that I had every intention of you never having the opportunity of hearing my voice again," I said.

"Listen, bro, I'm embarrassed by all of this . . . the words I said to you, the way I acted. All of it was out of character. I was in a very dark place. You have to know that."

Forgiveness was a winding road. It takes great patience and a keen sense of alertness to navigate its path. The pace in which one decides to forgive can potentially have a direct impact on its sincerity. For one who forgives too quickly, it could simply just be empty words for the sake of saying one forgives. However, with time and deep thought, you truly allow the heart to heal. I now understand the meaning of the saying, *Time heals all wounds.*

"Let's not pretend that those words didn't hold some type of validity for what you truly thought of me, Jackson. Let's not play that game."

"Bro, come on, man. We have a history, one that was built on a solid foundation. I admit I let the petty bullshit cloud my better judgment. I was jealous. Okay, I admit it."

His admission of jealously didn't sway my feelings one bit. I intended to forgive, not rekindle a broken friendship or brotherhood.

"You know, for the past couple of months, I've been thinking about all of this shit. I'm speaking about life. Life is a complicated muthafucka. In its complications, I've been able to find some type of normalcy within it. So, this shit between you and me represents the complicated. The normalcy represents my life now without you in it. So, while I accept your position of being honest and forgive you for what you've done, let's not get it twisted. Things will never be the same."

"I can respect that," said Jackson.

The tone in which he said it sounded as if a deflation of energy had been exchanged over the phone. I knew the tone all too well. It was a tone that tapped into his vulnerability. Being the true salesman that I am, I pounced on the opportunity to ask the question that I'd been wanting to ask. No longer tense. The residue of nervousness had since been removed. I now controlled the conversation as a puppet master would.

"Did you have me shot me?"

There was an awkward silence between us. It was as if fate had boxed us in, and there was no escape from the truth. I continued to hold in anticipation of what would come. How would I react? Was I truly ready for the answer?

***

When I left the park, I received a text from Natalie indicating that we needed to talk. I've grown accustomed to what *we need to talk* meant when it involved the women in my life. I wondered what I could have possibly done within the past couple of days that could have prompted "the talk." I mentally retraced my steps and said to myself, *I took out the trash in the bathroom. I didn't drink her water last night. No dishes were left in the sink because Grammy washed them. And most importantly, I've had no interactions whatsoever with anybody from the female anatomy who wasn't related to me other than Natalie or a member of the medical community.* Laughing to myself, I felt like the little boy who was waiting for his mother to get off work to see if he was getting a whooping when she got home. *This is childish and ridiculous*, I said to myself. *I'm a grown-ass man.*

I'd had an empty feeling since my conversation with Jackson; my emotions were still on an intensified level. I didn't have time for any more bullshit. He said he had nothing to do with my shooting. I'd gotten the answer that I needed to cleanse my mind. It wasn't necessarily a shock, but now, I needed to understand how I would proceed in my journey. Was my forgiveness an empty one? Did it hold true value? There were still more dots that I needed to connect, but for now, I had to put all of that on hold and deal with the issue at hand with Natalie—whatever that is.

As I approached the coffee shop we'd agreed to meet at, I told the Uber driver to drop me off a block away from the spot. I wanted to walk a little. Not just for the exercise physically but mentally. I had to take mental notes on what to expect. I didn't want to walk into a trap. Maybe it was just a talk to make things better. Maybe I didn't have a reason to expect the worst.

As I gingerly stepped out of the sedan, I thanked the driver for allowing me to have my cheat smoke in the backseat. He replied by giving me a pound and a smile that indicated that my secret was safe with him. Damaged lung or not, a cigarette every now and then is a luxury I am not ready to eliminate. My leg was a little weak because of my positioning in the car. I stopped and leaned against the storefront of a women's boutique Lisa and I used to frequently visit on weekends when we had time for each other. She loved the pink and green color scheme of the renovated building, and we used to always talk about opening a small shop like this in a small town and just enjoying life together.

When I gathered enough strength to make my journey, I pushed on. I pushed on past the man on the phone in his business suit, discussing what I perceived to be a huge business deal. I pushed on past the couple who seemed to be in serious disagreement about where they would eat. I pushed on past the kid on his bicycle who was sneakily looking at the asses of every woman he rode past. I pushed on until I was at my destination.

When I entered the establishment, I looked it over in search of Natalie. My expectations had long been forgotten on my walk, and I was ready for anything at this point. Nothing surprised me anymore. My search ended when I saw her ducked off inside a cozy corner near the unisex restroom. She was sitting still. Her face was rather stoic; deep in thought. I sighed and made my way. I greeted the young lady at the counter as I declined her offer to order one of the "fancy" coffees of the season. I approached. Our eyes met. I put my cane on the seat of the booth and extended my arms toward her and asked, "So, how was your day?"

It was the open-ended question that would allow me to gauge how this conversation would ultimately go. For better or worse, it was either going to be more complications or the normalcy in life I was chasing. Jackson was the complicated bullshit. Where would Natalie be placed?

Chapter 7

Natalie

I saw him, and my heart melted. Here he was broken and on the mend but doing the best he could. Fuck that bitch. I don't care what she said; Marcus is *my* man. We live in the same house, and we share a healthy, happy child. We weren't together when he said those things . . . *if* he said those things. We'd both spent too much time dwelling on the past, and this is our future, and we are going to make it glorious. No Chanel, no Jackson, and no Lisa. Just Natalie, Marcus, and Trenton, our imperfect triangle.

"So, how was your day?" he asked. He was sweating. No doubt from the struggle steps it took for him to get into the restaurant. He also smelled like cigarettes, and I wondered if he had been smoking. I shook my head. I wasn't going to give him another struggle, not today, anyway. He was wearing gray sweatpants, and I loved it when he wore gray sweatpants because when he turned to just the right angle, I could see the outline of his manhood. I smiled as he angled himself.

I stood up and hugged him. "I love you, Marcus Colbert," I said and fell into his arms. We held each other tightly for a few seconds, and he nuzzled my neck with his nose and then kissed me on my neck. Once we released, I ran my hand over his scruffy beard, which he hadn't shaved in weeks, but I actually found it sexy. Then, I pulled his face to mine and kissed him slowly and tenderly. At first, he seemed hesitant, but then he returned the kiss and pulled me further into him. Our bodies bonded to one another's like magnets. And I suddenly felt a familiar friend rise to greet me. I laughed. He whispered in my ear, "I thought you wanted to talk." I bit his earlobe and sucked it gently before I said, "I did, but I wouldn't be opposed to doing something else if you are."

He smiled his devilish grin and said, "I don't mind at all."

I smiled back. "Then, I'll go get the car." He tasted like cigarette smoke. We would talk about the dangers of smoking in his condition later. I had something else more important on my mind.

I drove the car to the front of the restaurant; he got in and smiled at me. I could see his manhood bulging against the soft fabric. I'd missed him so much. We couldn't go to Marcus' condo because Grammy was there. I still had my apartment, so we decided to go there. I'd been so busy with Marcus and the baby that I hadn't had time to pack and move my things to storage, so it was less of a hassle to pay the rent until I had time to do so. Luckily, my apartment was close. Once we got inside, we ripped each other's clothes off like madmen. Even though he hadn't worked out in months, Marcus still had a slight build on him. I guess he had heredity to thank for that. I knew I had to be careful with him, as he was still fragile and simple tasks could cause him large amounts of pain. I told him to lie back and relax, and he obeyed without hesitation.

I looked at the scars from surgery on his chest and slowly kissed the length of each one. Then I straddled him and rode his thick manhood slowly and lovingly. I didn't want to hurt him, but I needed him to feel me as much as I needed to feel him. I thanked the heavens that this part of him still worked wonderfully. I rode his length like a little girl who was finally tall enough to get on the ride at the fair she had been coveting for years. It had probably been six months or more since we made love. I had my pregnancy, his relationship with Chanel, and his recovery to blame for that. Tears began to stream down my cheeks. I loved this man more than I loved myself. I was almost in disbelief that finally, I had him all to myself. He finally recognized me and treated me as his woman. The woman he wanted to build a life with, and I didn't care if he was broken or 100 percent; I would take him any way I could get him. I knew God was going to restore him to his former self, and everything would be fine. I let out a moan of pleasure, and then I heard Marcus softly say my name before releasing a moan of his own. "Say you love me," I said. "I need to hear you say it."

"I—love—you—Natalie." The words were barely audible as the ecstasy we were both feeling consumed his body. Then I felt both our sexual tensions melt away simultaneously. Shit. We didn't use a condom. Oh well. I stared down at him before gently lowering my body next to his.

After a few minutes, while basking in the afterglow, Marcus said, "I love you, Natalie. I really do love you. I wanted to say it again so you would know I wasn't just caught up in the moment. I know I haven't been the easiest person to deal with, but I am truly grateful for the way you have stayed by my side and supported me while I work my way back."

I snuggled my naked body against his and looked him in his eyes. Right there in the captivating brown of his irises, I saw LOVE and SINCERITY. "There's no place else I'd rather be," I said. "I love you, too."

He kissed me and then said, "Natalie Tellis, will you marry me?"

I blinked hard and then stared at him in disbelief. I had to be dreaming. Let me check.

"What did you say?"

"I said, 'Natalie Tellis, will you marry me?'" He kissed my lips again.

"Yes, baby, I will marry you!" I screamed and then planted several kisses all over his adorable face, with the last one landing squarely on his lips. I was going to be his wife!

"Good. Now let me give you something, the future Mrs. Natalie Colbert." He kissed me once more on my lips and then on my neck. He planted another one in between my breasts, and the next one was on the right nipple, followed by one on the left. He sucked on it, and I think he forgot I was breastfeeding. A little milk came out, and he licked it up. "It's sweet," he said.

I giggled and said, "So, I hear. Stop. That's for our baby."

"I was your baby before he was." His eyes gleamed with mischief.

Marcus then went back to his task and slowly made his way down in spite of the pain I knew he was feeling until he reached my treasure chest. He performed what I had come to call a "Colbert Special."

When he finished, I could barely move. He looked around. "This place is dusty. No one is here. We're wasting money having two places. We have to move you out of here soon. You and everything you own belongs at home with Trenton and me. I hope you haven't been keeping this place to escape to if I get too out of hand. I know I've been selfish. This is hard for me." He pointed his finger at his chest and made a circle in the air to emphasize his point. "This wasn't how I imagined starting our lives together. Coming back from the dead isn't easy. I don't want our son to grow up and see me in this position. My father was always my symbol of strength and manhood. Even in his old age, he's still my role model and the kind of man I aspire to be. What if I can't run with my son or throw the ball around in the yard?"

He sure knew how to ruin an orgasmic high. I reached over and grabbed his hand. "I know this has been hard for you, baby. I understand, and I'm here for you every step of the way. I am certain by the time Trenton learns to walk, you will have made a full recovery or at least be close to it. You will be the kind of father you have always wanted to be. I pray for you every night, and I'm sure God hears me, and He will answer favorably."

"I hope so," he said. Marcus gazed off for a moment, and then he smiled. "Look at me, ruining the mood. Let's change the subject. You were great, by the way. I got my very own cowgirl. Yee-Haaa!" he said while twirling an imaginary lasso. We both laughed. It was good to laugh again, together. It wasn't something we did very often these days. He kissed me and squeezed my breast. "You really are beautiful, Natalie."

I was completely naked, breasts bare and swollen with milk. My large, brown nipples were sore and a little red from the greedy suckling baby who latched on so tightly that sometimes I wanted to snatch the part of my anatomy that provided nourishment back. I needed to pump before I went back to work to relieve that achingly full feeling I had become familiar with. My stretch-marked abdomen was in full visibility as a reminder of the child I carried and gave birth to. I hadn't lost all my baby weight, and I was thick, to say the least. My large thighs and buttocks could have graced the cover of any black porn magazine. Yet, even in my imperfect state, I felt more beautiful than I ever had. I loved that Marcus thought I was beautiful, too.

I had just made love to my man who thought he had another child on the way with another woman. I bet he performed those Colbert Specials on Chanel, and that was why she wanted him back so badly. The thought made my stomach ache.

Marcus took his finger and traced my stretch marks with his index finger. "I'm going to be a better man for you—for us. You deserve it. We'll go pick you out a ring this weekend. I also promise not to let my situation with Chanel impede our happiness. I will be a great father to both children and an amazing husband to you. I promise. Now, what did you want to talk about?"

My first reaction was to say nothing. Yet, it was hiding secrets and lies that started our problems and placed such distrust between us. I had to go ahead and tell him. Hell, he just proposed. It wasn't like Marcus was going to take it back.

"I saw Chanel today," I said slowly.

"Oh," he said with his mouth while his eyes searched mine for silent answers, any hint that my demeanor might give to what I was about to say. I laid there silently for a moment before I continued.

"Yes, she asked me to meet her for lunch. She wanted me to deliver a message to you. She couldn't face you herself."

"Okay. What is it? She betta not be trying to start any shit."

I answered his question as fast as I could before I changed my mind about telling the truth.

"She wanted me to tell you that she lost the baby, and she never wants to hear from you or see you again."

Marcus removed his hand from my body and stared at me. I waited for his full reaction to the news I delivered. After a few seconds, he tore his eyes away from me and looked at the ceiling above us. The love that was previously in his eyes was replaced with pain. I always wondered how he felt about Chanel having his baby. We never really discussed it, but now I knew he wanted that child with her.

"This is my fault," he said. "I should have been there for her, but I couldn't. When I find out who shot me, they will pay." A dark cloud covered his face, and that pain morphed into something else. His eyes held an anger I had never seen before. With his rugged afro, scruffy facial hairs and menacing expression, Marcus looked almost like a demon. A sexy demon but a demon, nonetheless.

My heart dropped, and I immediately wished I had lied. The beautiful, loving connection we created in my dusty, uninhabited apartment had been abruptly severed with invisible scissors. My husband-to-be got up, slid his sweatpants on, and went into the bathroom. I heard him turn on the faucet and let the water run into the sink. I walked to the door, pressed my ear against it, and strained to hear the sobs for another woman's child Marcus didn't want me to witness. I gathered my clothes and went to the bathroom in the hallway to get ready to go back to work. It was the one place in my life where I didn't mind having to compete with others.

Chapter 8

Marcus

Truth. Many of us spend most of our lives chasing it—willing to embrace it. However, the truth is that when we do find what we're looking for, it tends to leave us open. Open for hurt. Hence, the truth hurts. I heard a soft knock on the bathroom door. I turned off the faucet that had been running for the past ten minutes to act as a shield for the guiltiness that trailed down my eyes. I could hear my mother's voice saying, *Boy, if you don't turn that damned faucet off wasting good water, I'm gonna waste my strength with this belt.* It's funny how insignificant memories can curl up your mouth in inauspicious times.

"Just a minute," I yelled. I grabbed the nearest towel and proceeded to wash away any remains of Chanel that could be seen with the naked eye. I opened the door and saw Natalie standing there. She was fully dressed. She'd placed her hair in a ponytail, eyes round and direct, lips freshly glossed, and I smelled a cinnamon-type fragrance that was pleasing my senses.

"I'm headed back to work." She said it as if we hadn't just shared one of the most intimate times in our relationship. We both seemed to be accustomed to masking our pain. Maybe it was the pregnancy or sympathy she felt for me for not being fully myself. Nevertheless, she was growing, maturing in our relationship.

"So soon?" I asked. Hoping that she would say no and decide to stay so that we could talk things out, I wanted to try a different approach. Then again, maybe she needed to leave. Maybe this was her way of coping to avoid another argument.

She pondered for a moment with her lips pulled in as if she were fighting the urge to say something. She nodded. "Yes. I think I should." She released a small sigh. "Do you want me to give you a ride somewhere or back home?"

Progress. Previously, we would have been at each other's throats. Me saying words I couldn't take back, and her releasing her venom with an intent to injure and infect every ego muscle within my body. I studied her a little more before I replied, "I think I'll stay here awhile—if that's okay with you?"

"Stay as long as you like. Today may be a late day at work, so I'll see you tonight?"

She had asked as if I had no intentions of going to the home we now shared. Maybe she was studying me as well to see if I had grown, matured in our relationship. Maybe she was yearning and needed more clarity on the feelings I had for Chanel. Maybe she just needed that reassurance. I could have easily embraced her and grabbed her face, to let her know that she was now my one and only and allowed our tongues to do the talking as they intertwined in a way that relieved the unwanted tension between us. But I didn't. So, she left. She left without that reassurance. I sent her back out into a world of the unknown with self-doubts—a world that was a dangerous potion for her and me. A world that had pushed her to someone like Jackson.

"Will you do me one favor?" she asked before exiting.

"Anything," I said.

"Don't smoke here. The smell lingers for days."

I was busted, and I braced myself for the tongue-lashing that was coming.

Instead, Natalie just looked at me solemnly, shook her head, and left. I wondered if that meant she didn't care or if she was just fed up with my shit.

The pain of knowing that Chanel had to suffer through that ordeal alone got the best of me. After Natalie left, I understood why. I understood and respected the fact that she would allow me the time and space to let this settle within my head. I hated the fact that it ruined the intimacy that we shared that afternoon in her apartment.

I stayed for another hour or so backtracking and thinking about the last conversation Chanel and I had. I paced back and forth without my cane. I paced past the readers' nest of books that was sitting in the middle of the hallway. I paced past the abundance of opened and unopened mail stuffed inside an old shoebox. I paced past the large crack in the wall that used to be a place-holder for what seemed to be the dinosaur remains of a telephone. I paced past and walked over the numerous half-chewed, fabric torn, once slobbery toys that belonged to Pepper. It hurt but I didn't care. As I paced by it all, that feeling of emptiness that I once had returned. I was also tired as hell. My physical therapist would appreciate that I took the initiative to get some exercise though.

I didn't want to spend too much time having a pity party for myself. Part of my recovery treatment entailed learning different coping mechanisms that allowed for positive results. Up until the point when I was shot, so much of my life had been predicated toward me coping with issues one way—closed-ended. Meaning, I didn't always take responsibility for my actions. I sought out ways to justify my reactions, no matter who was on the receiving end of the hurt or confusion. Albeit, some of the issues I found myself in weren't my fault exclusively. I didn't always respond in a conducive way, however. I decided to reach out to my therapist, who had done a phenomenal job helping me to recover. Luckily, she was available.

"Dr. Ward, I appreciate you taking the time to take my call," I said. Dr. Ward and I had built quite the doctor-patient relationship. I tried not to abuse her willingness to talk with me anytime. I tried not to call outside our appointments unless I truly needed it. And I wondered if I was keeping her from something important.

"So, are your legs catching up to your brain, yet?" She laughed at our inside joke. During one of our sessions, I had foolishly attempted to diagnose myself by studying every depressive topic via Google.

After sharing the chuckle with her, I replied, "I'm feeling better by the day. I know that this could have probably waited until my appointment next week, but I need someone to vent to. I would also like to add that I've been trying out the new coping technique we discussed during my last visit."

"Fabulous," she said. I could envision her saying it while leaning over the desk with her thick dark hair draped over her shoulders, bright eyed with her full lips spread wide open displaying a perfect set of white teeth. "So, what's the heartbeat of the situation?"

I knew that was going to be the next question. I loved that question, mostly because it forces me to sift through the rubbish and get to the issue at hand. "That dark cloud is hovering over me, again," I said.

"So, I see," she said. She said it so exact, so definitive as if she were the sole key holder to my treasures of pain, sorrow, and guilt. A place I hoped Natalie would be in one day. "What do you think that is?"

"Honestly, I don't think I deserve to be in a healthy relationship. It seems like the harder I try, the more shit arises to bring me back, as if God is teasing me with the taste of chocolate only to deny me the entire bar."

She laughed. "I don't mean to laugh at you. Truly, I don't. But you have the most vivid imagination with your sayings." She cleared her throat. "So, you don't think you deserve the necessities of love since you haven't been able to experience the type of love that was taken from you in the form of Lisa? That is the only relationship that you can revert to where the ending had nothing to do with what you did. You must get past that, Marcus. As I've said before, in order for you to move forward, you must get past your past. How are you sleeping at night?"

"It's been sporadic. The medication helps."

"Well, let's not get too dependent on that."

"You have no fight from me on that one. Trust me," I said.

"How are things going with the investigation? Any new thoughts, revelations?"

"I spoke with *him* today."

She knew who I was referring to. Having that conversation with Jackson did relieve some of the stress I was feeling from that situation. I'll admit that it is scary to be in a world where there is potentially someone still out there lurking, looking for an opportunity to end your life.

"Wow. That's major progress. How was it?"

I could hear her scribbling in her notepad. The background noise had now been muted on her side, which indicated that she was fully vested in our conversation.

"It was awkward at first, but I asked him for honesty about the things that transpired between us, and he was. At least, I think he was."

"That's good," she said. She waited to see if I was going to divulge exactly what we discussed. When I didn't, she said, "How is the investigation going?"

"It's been an uneasy road; still no fresh leads or new information from the police. There is still a strong case of paranoia on my part."

"It's going to take some time. You have experienced a handful of traumatic episodes in a short spurt of time. How open are you about it with Natalie? The paranoia, I'm speaking of."

"I don't speak too much on it. I don't want to seem weak."

I heard more jotting and scribbling.

"I see," she replied. Sometimes when she replied with an *I see,* she would lean back in her chair, cross her left leg over the right, with her ink pen seductively teasing from her mouth while she studied me. "Why do you see that as a sign of weakness? I mean, vulnerability is one of the paths toward healing, especially with the one you supposedly love."

She'd said it. She was questioning the love I have for Natalie. Was I not convincing enough in the way I feel about her? Most importantly, have I been convincing to Natalie? Does she really know that I love her? Sure. I've told her, but did she feel it, believe it? I mean, hell, I just asked her to marry me, for heaven's sake.

I had an incoming call interrupting my session with Dr. Ward. "Excuse me for a minute, Dr. Ward," I said before clicking over.

The voice on the other end said, "Where are you? I thought you were at home."

It was my sister. I had forgotten about the meet-up we were supposed to have. I was so inundated with the weight of my personal issues, that I was overlooking the problematic issues that were building within the walls of my immediate family, starting with my sister. We had a long overdue conversation that needed to be had.

"I'm sorry, Mia. Don't leave. Give me about thirty minutes to an hour, and I'll be home."

After apologizing again, I clicked back over to Dr. Ward.

"Sorry about that. Where were we?"

"I was asking about your level of vulnerability and your unwillingness to open it up to anyone that you say you love. I mean, you've opened up to me. Why not Natalie?"

That was the million-dollar question. However, it wasn't entirely true. There were times that I did allow Natalie to enter that vulnerable place, no matter how limited.

"I guess a part of it is the fact that you and I have a no-judgment zone. I don't feel as if you'll judge me based on my experiences: past, present, or future. That doesn't mean I don't love you, though."

I enjoyed talking and joking with Dr. Ward. I honestly think that as much as she was helping me, I was helping her as well; she was experiencing relationship issues, too. She and her husband of fifteen years recently divorced. She disclosed this information to me in one of our more intimate sessions. Unprofessional as it might have been, that made me open up more to her. She seemed more real. I no longer looked at her as just someone who was trying to make me better. I looked at her as something more. I don't know what that more represents, but it isn't sexual, even though she is "prime time" and someone I would normally date. She's attractive, ambitious, and assertive. She is the total package of what sexy represents to me.

She chuckled as she replied, "Well, that's nice to hear. So, tell me more about . . ."

I told her about Chanel losing the baby and my feelings about it. I told her that I proposed to Natalie, and I allowed myself to share my innermost thoughts and emotions with her . . . the things I couldn't or wouldn't share with Natalie. Our conversation continued and faded within the confidentiality that we shared.

Chapter 9

Natalie

He just found out he lost a child. He just found out he lost a child. He just found out he lost a child. I kept telling myself that repeatedly as I maneuvered my way through the congested Nashville interstate back to work downtown. He lost a life, a human being who never had a chance to enter the world or reach his or her full potential. Marcus had every right to grieve the loss of that life. Now that I'd had some time to think about the events of the day, I realized how insensitive I was to Chanel. She lost her child as well. As a new mother, I couldn't imagine not having Trenton. I felt God tugging on my heart to apologize. I didn't want to call that woman; she had wreaked so much havoc in my life, but I had to be obedient. God had a way of whooping my behind when I didn't.

My phone synched to my car's Bluetooth when I got in, so I instructed it to call Chanel. I didn't expect her to answer, but she did. "I'm sorry," I blurted out before she had a chance to say anything other than hello. "I'm sorry you lost your baby. I know none of this has been easy for you, and I also apologize for being so insensitive earlier. As a woman who has carried life, I know losing your child must have been devastating. I also apologize for any hurt that I caused you out of my own anger or pain. I know you didn't mean for any of this to happen. As you said, we loved the same man, and that's where things took a turn for the worst."

It was quiet on the other end for a few seconds, then Chanel let out a very low, "Thank you. You have no idea the unimaginable pain I feel. I found comfort in knowing that even if Marcus wouldn't love me, our child would. I never even got a chance to show him the ultrasound or tell Marcus I was having a boy. I was going to name him Marquis. I figured in time, we would all put away our differences, and our children would form an unbreakable bond. I am an only child, so I don't know what it's like to have siblings."

I thought about Jessie. "It has its ups and downs, but it's a strong bond. You would do almost anything for them," I said. *Even lie, keep secrets, and hide evidence.*

"I bet. Can I tell you something?"

"Sure."

"While Marcus was in the hospital, Jackson started calling me."

"What?"

"Yeah, girl. He tried to be my shoulder to lean on in time of need."

I chuckled. Same ole Jackson.

"I almost went for it. I almost did what Marcus did with me and choose an alternative to the one I really wanted. I mean, I'm sorry. I didn't mean that like it came out."

This chick was a piece of work, but I wanted to hear the rest of her dealings with Jackson, so I let her comment slide. "It's okay. Now, what were you saying about Jackson?"

"Well, tell Marcus to stay away from that man. I have a discerning spirit. There's a darkness lurking underneath that suave exterior. He's a snake in a tailor-made suit. I'd go so far to say he has an evil spirit in him.

He told me you two were close at one time, and I have a feeling you still are. You should stay away from him as well. He means you no good."

Jackson had his less-than-desirable qualities, but I wouldn't go so far as to say he was evil. He'd been very good to me. I owed this new job with a great salary and room for advancement to him. "Yes, Jackson can be conniving, but he's always been kind to me. A true friend," I said.

"There is good in him, and I sensed that as well, but there is something else there. I couldn't put my finger on it but stay away from him. TRUST ME on that one. God gave me a gift; I know evil when I see it, no matter how hard people try to mask it."

As I continued to drive and listen, I wondered if there was any validity to what Chanel stated about evil lurking inside him. I knew Jackson had some insecurities and jealousy when it came to Marcus, but I never sensed anything evil. Right then, I resolved to cut all ties with Jackson. No more money, no more use of his connections, and I had to fully dedicate myself to the man who needed me the most. I was going to do something special for him tonight to try to cheer him up. My man needed me, and I would be there for him. If Jackson was indeed evil, I had to protect him as well.

Chapter 10

Marcus

"Auntie to the rescue?" I teased Mia as I witnessed her trying to settle Trenton down as he was having one of his mid-afternoon wailing sessions. Now sitting down next to them, I reached over to grab the little fella, placed him snugly in my arms, and began to hum one of his favorite tunes from Disney. For some reason, that seemed to calm him down. It might have been the awful off-key tunes I was making that did the trick.

"Where's Momma and Grammy?" I asked.

"Momma took her to the store to pick up some of her medication and grab some things for dinner. I think they're making spaghetti or something like that. As hungry as I am, it doesn't matter what they make—I'm feeding my face to the max."

Now making silly faces at Trenton, I replied in one of my character voices, "Ain't yo' daddy such a lucky guy to have him some of Momma's special spaghetti today?" In between his cooing, I continued, "Yes, I am. Yes, I am."

"You are going to be a great father, Marcus," said Mia.

"What makes you so sure of that?"

"I can just tell. When you are around Trenton, you get that same special glow that Dad always has when he's with us."

"Welp, if I can muster up to be half the man he is, then I guess I won't end up too bad. Ain't that right, lil' fella?" I received Trenton's approval via the slobbery string that was trailing from his mouth to my shirt. "So, what's been up with you, Mia? How's school going?"

She sighed slightly and replied, "I guess you can say that everything is cool."

"You don't sound too confident. Be real with me, what's the deal?"

She stood up and began to move around like she always did when she felt as if she were about to be interrogated.

"I mean, there is not too much to tell. I work. I go to class. And basically, that's it. Especially since I no longer have a car. There really ain't much more I can do."

"How are things going with the whole counseling thing?"

"It's going. I mean, after what happened to you, I just—"

Her face began to twitch up, which meant that tears would soon follow. Still holding Trenton in my arms, I motioned for her to sit next to me. As she lay her head on my shoulder, I replied, "It's okay, Mia. I'm okay."

"I don't know what I would have done if I had lost you."

"I'm still here, Sis. I'm still here," I said as I continued to console her. "Now, as your big brother, you know I must also get all up in your business, right?"

She lifted her head from my shoulder and wiped away a trailed off tear. "I know that. I guess you've been talking to Natalie about me, huh?" she said between sniffs.

"Yes. I've heard some things. They all weren't necessarily from Nat, but Momma as well. So, what's up?"

"I mean, it wasn't no big deal or nothing. I think they both were just blowing things out of proportion."

"Well, let me be that judge of that. What were the things they were blowing out of proportion?"

I could tell that it had something to do with boys because her face began to redden up a bit.

"It's hard to talk about this stuff with you," she said as she twisted her thumbs. "Can we just change the subject, please?"

"Trust me, this is just as uncomfortable for me as it is for you, but I need to know that you're okay."

She remained silent for a second. Trenton interrupted the empty silence with his playful cooing . . . or maybe he wanted to know the details as well.

"I was using the car to go and see this guy I was dating at Middle Tennessee State University."

"Was?" I asked.

"Yes, was."

"So, how old was this guy?"

"Twenty-two," she mumbled.

"Twenty-two?" I asked for confirmation.

"Wasn't Cynthia like twenty-four when you were seventeen or eighteen?"

"Don't try to turn this around on me. How did you meet this guy?"

"I mean, you did it. I don't see the big deal. It's not like I didn't know what I was doing, or he was controlling me, or some crazy stuff like that."

"Are you having sex?" I had finally asked the question as it felt weird escaping my lips. It was probably the most uncomfortable I'd been in quite some time, and I didn't necessarily want to know as I cringed at the thought of my little sister having sex, but with me being a guy and knowing the things I'd done to other people's little sisters, I just wanted some assurance that she was at least using protection and not being out in these streets being a little too hot to the point where her reputation could bring negative energy her way.

Surprised by my question, she replied, "Marcus? I can't believe you asked me that." Her face was now as red as the pasta sauce my momma would soon be making.

"Look, all I ask is that you be smart with your decisions. I'm not naive enough to think that while you're growing up, you won't face these types of situations. I just want to be certain that you don't put yourself in predicaments that could potentially bring harm your way."

She nodded before she placed the pillow over her face to hide the shame of having a sex talk with her big brother.

"Was this guy your first? Did you use protection?"

"Ughhhh. You're killing me right now. I can't believe you're asking me this." She slowly removed the pillow from her face and continued, "I've only been with two guys—including him, and, yes, we used protection. Now, can we *please* change the subject?"

I could have pressed her some more, but I didn't want to become too overbearing. I allowed the conversation to navigate toward another subject. Now that we've had some conversation about her life decisions, it would be easier for us to have these conversations moving forward.

Chapter 11

Natalie

To say I had mixed feelings would be an understatement. My body was elated to have finally gotten some attention. It was goooood too! I was already craving some more, and it hadn't been a full four hours since I'd seen Marcus. However, my mind was in a tailspin. It was wanting to exhibit some sympathy for a man who'd lost a child while wanting the same man to not care so deeply about a woman he wasn't with and a child he didn't conceive with me. Did it make me a bad person to be a little happy that I wouldn't have to contend with a bastard stepson and his pining-for-my-man mother? I tried not to focus on it as I continued to work on the Waterhouse Publishing account.

At about 5:00 p.m., Shari called my desk phone to let me know that I had a delivery. "Should I bring them to you?" she asked.

"Them? No, I'll come to you." The people in my office were nosy enough as it was. I didn't need them asking a million questions about who gave me what and why. As I rounded the corner to her desk, three large beautiful bouquets of white roses accosted me.

Shari was smiling as if she had been given the roses. "Somebody loves you," she cooed.

"It would appear so." I buried my face in several of them and inhaled their sweet scent. "We should all take time to smell the roses," I said after removing my face from them.

"I concur. The card is in this one," she said while pointing to the roses in a red vase on the far side of her desk. The other two were in clear vases.

I found the small red envelope and opened it to find written in handwriting I didn't recognize, "LET'S PICK UP WHERE WE LEFT OFF. MEET ME TONIGHT AT 7:00 P.M. WEAR SOMETHING SEXY OR NOTHING AT ALL. DON'T WORRY ABOUT ANYTHING. I'VE TAKEN CARE OF EVERYTHING."

The envelope also contained an electronic key card for the Lamden Plaza Hotel. Marcus could be so romantic when he wanted to. It was now about 5:10, which didn't give me much time to get sexy. If I leave now, I could go to my apartment to get dolled up, and I didn't want to go to the condo because if I go home and see my son, I might not want to leave. Besides, Marcus said he had taken care of everything. I would call Grammy on the way to the hotel to check on things. We could use a night away from everyone. Just me and my man like it used to be.

***

I arrived at the hotel about 6:55 p.m. I tried to call Grammy a couple of times, but her cell phone kept going to voicemail. I chuckled at the thought of how she balked at the idea of getting a cell phone, but since she discovered games like Candy Crush and Casino, you almost had to pry it away from her. She probably let the battery die. Sometimes, Grammy forgets that she needs to charge the thing regularly for it to operate properly. I would ask Marcus about her and Trenton when I saw him.

I took the elevator up to room 755. The walls were mirrored, and I inspected myself to make sure my makeup and hair were flawless. I was wearing sexy black lingerie underneath a long pink trench coat. This was the first time I'd worn this ensemble from Frederick's of Hollywood. It was a little snug because of the weight I'd gained, but I didn't anticipate having it on long. I knocked on the door, and when no one answered, I used the key I'd been given to open it. The lights in the room were dim; white candles were strategically placed around the spacious suite containing a king-size bed; and the covers were pulled back with red rose petals sprinkled on the crisp white sheets adorning what appeared to be a very plush mattress. I could hear someone in the bathroom, so I announced my arrival with a simple, "Baby, I'm here."

No answer. I walked over to the bed, and an envelope lay on it. I got closer and read the words on the envelope. "*Read Me*," what was this Alice in Wonderland? I opened the envelope and inside was a piece of white paper with the words *"Silence is all that is required. Where we're going, words are not needed. Lie down and close your eyes. When you open them, you'll get a surprise."* I liked the sound of that, but there better be plenty of moaning and groaning intermingled in that silence. I took off my trench coat and laid it on the back of a chair sitting near a small desk. I then went back to the bed and tried to situate myself in a seductive pose. I made sure my thigh-high panty hose and black stiletto heels were free of any debris before grabbing my breasts and pushing them up to give them a little more lift than my push-up bra was providing. Then, I closed my eyes and waited. I heard the bathroom door open, and Marcus approaching the bed. I felt soft but unfamiliar lips on top of mine. I opened my eyes and what I saw sucked all the breath from my lungs. I wanted to scream, but no sound escaped. I diverted my eyes from the naked being in front of me with a full erection.

"Jackson! What the fuck are you doing here?!" I squeaked out.

"It's obvious, isn't it? You've been playing with me for months, dangling this sexy ass in front of me just enough to get me to help you. Well, it's time to pay the piper," he said.

"I never meant to tease you. I thought you understood we were just friends."

I scrambled off the bed, retrieved my coat, and quickly put it on. "Jackson, please put some pants on. This isn't going to happen."

He continued to stand there with a hard-on. The man was blessed, but I wasn't interested at all. I had a man who was even more endowed, and he was all I needed and wanted.

"So you let your friends pay your bills, go down on you, and get you employment making a salary you would never have otherwise? That doesn't sound like a friendship to me. Sounds like something your man would do. Why do you resist what was meant to be?" He sat down on the edge of the bed.

I sat down on the chair with my trench coat on, hoping I could reason with him. I felt a little more comfortable now that there was some space between us. I tried hard to divert my eyes from his penis, which was pointed in my direction. "I'm with Marcus. We have a child," I said.

"You mean the one I was helping you to care for while Marcus was laid up?"

I sighed. "If this is about money I'll pay back every cent. I promise."

Jackson cocked his head to the side and looked at me as if I were slow. "You don't get it. So let me explain it to you. You are going to make love to me tonight because you're screwed in more ways than one. How are you going to explain to anyone that you came to my hotel room in your underwear, and you didn't intend to have sex with me? No one will believe you. Also, if you are stupid enough to attempt to tell someone, I will not only get you fired from that job you love so much, but I'll call the police and tell them what your brother and Manny did to Marcus. So, all in one moment of defiance, you are going to lose your man because I guarantee Marcus will never believe you didn't come here to give yourself to me willingly. You will also lose your livelihood, your brother, and your best friend. Think about it. All you have to do is to spread those thick thighs for me this one time. You never know, you might like it. By the way, I took pictures of you while you had your eyes closed and you were lying across the bed."

"You're crazy. This is blackmail!" I said.

"Honey, you have no idea, and I owe my insanity to you. I lost my fiancée, you, my best friend, and then I lost my mind. Marcus actually thinks I had him shot him. Yes, we had some competition going, but I never wanted to kill him."

I sat there contemplating what I was going to do. This was my punishment for not ending our friendship when Marcus told me to.

"I only have to do this once, and you'll leave me alone forever?" I asked softly.

"That's what I said. You are in no position to negotiate, Natalie. Why you hoes refuse me but welcome that runt with open arms is beyond me. It's time I get something I want. I'm handsome, I'm successful, and rich. You should be begging me to make love to you. Now, get that sexy phat ass of yours over here and lie across this bed like you would if I were Marcus!"

I didn't move. I was in a no-win situation. Jackson had me cornered in every way imaginable. He was right. No one would believe me if I told them the truth. Marcus would leave me, and my brother and Manny would go to jail. Jackson had the power to take away everything I held dear except my son, but how would I support Trenton with no job?

Jackson came over to me, knelt, and began kissing my neck. He put his hand in my coat and began fondling my breasts. I continued to sit there wondering what to do.

"Relax. I promise I'll be gentle," he said in between kisses. He stood up and extended his hand toward me, waiting for me to take it and join him on the bed. I looked at the large cross he had tattooed on the right side of his chest, bit my bottom lip, shut my eyes tightly, and prayed for this nightmare to end. What had I gotten myself into? *Dear God, please deliver me.*

Chapter 12

Marcus

I was awakened by the sound of what seemed to be a car backfiring. I was used to the sound as it indicated that Mr. Roy was headed off to work his late shift. This was around the time that Trenton usually needed his "nightcap" for the night.

My head had been resting comfortably, near the window, wedged between the two fluffy pillows Grammy had bought for me upon my release from the hospital. She said that they would help ease the tension and potential soreness in my upper back and neck area. I glanced over at the alarm clock that read 10:18 p.m. For clarity, I grabbed my phone to confirm the time; it mirrored that of the alarm clock. I noticed that I had a couple of missed calls from 1-800 numbers, Facebook and Instagram notifications, and an alert from my Bible app, indicating that I needed to catch up with my reading plan.

The bed looked the same, the pillows sitting firmly against the headboard, sheets fitted to a tee, Natalie's teddy bear nestled in the middle, and Trenton's blanket draped over the foot. *Maybe she's in the living room watching television*, I said to myself. It was odd not seeing Natalie in the room, just getting out of the shower, hanging her bra on the bathroom doorknob, or falling asleep in the recliner that was conveniently located by the television. I can't recall how many times, I'd had to either place the bra where it should go or turn the television off and drape a blanket over a sleeping Natalie balled up in my recliner.

As I was exiting the room, I glanced over for any traces of Natalie—her purse on the nightstand, work clothes in a pile near the hamper, earrings hanging from her jewelry box, or keys on the hook. There was nothing. Pepper stirred from the spot on the bedroom floor where he was sleeping and trotted behind me looking around too as if he noticed that someone was missing as well. Why was that damn dog wearing pajamas? Mia must have put them on him.

When I entered the living room, Mia was asleep on the coach. No television, no sound. The lights from Trenton's toy truck, which he was too young to play with yet, were the only thing alert in the room. I keep forgetting to take the batteries out of that thing since it has no use now. Natalie's dinner that I left for her was still on the stove with a paper towel over it. I noticed Grammy's phone on the kitchen table, so I reached for it to see if she had received a call from Natalie, but the phone was like everything else in the house—dead asleep. As I was making my way back to the bedroom to grab my phone to call Natalie and check on Grammy and Trenton, I heard the front door begin to open with ease as if a criminal were making a grand but silent entrance. Pepper barked. If she was trying to make a silent entrance, her own dog ruined her plan.

"Hey! You startled me," Natalie said, clutching her purse and with one hand while holding the other over her chest as I made my way from behind the kitchen wall.

"Late night?" I asked.

She nervously began to fidget with her keys. "I-I just had to finish up some work."

I then thought about the exchange we had earlier in the day. *Maybe she needed some time to breathe and collect her thoughts*, I thought to myself. "Look, about earlier today, I'm—"

"It's okay," Natalie said, cutting me off.

Wanting to lighten up the mood a little, I positioned the conversation to learn more about her day. After all, this was a technique I was learning in therapy. If you can get someone to talk about themselves, you will usually get any answers you are looking for.

"How was your day? My mom and Grammy hooked up some bomb spaghetti, and I left some for you," I said as I pointed toward the stove. "Trenton nearly drooled over everything; I swear that kid knows how to leave his mark anytime and anyplace." I searched her face for some reaction . . . a smile? Maybe a giggle or a continuation of the conversation. Instead, all I received in return was a dry, "I'm about to shower up."

She then clutched her coat tightly around herself and walked clumsily toward the bedroom.

I gave her some time to get settled, but I knew something wasn't right. Something seemed off. After nearly an hour or so, I trailed to the bedroom. Everything seemed to be in place: purse on the nightstand, earrings hanging from her jewelry box, and keys on the hook; all except the pile of work clothes on the floor—they were not seen. She was in bed breathing soundly.

I started to take a shower myself, but my anxiety wouldn't allow me to. I began to peel away the light layers of clothing I had on and positioned myself inside the sheets, close to Natalie, her back against my chest, butt near my groin. She smelled sweeter than usual, as if she had bathed in multiple shower gels.

I reached around her thick frame to caress her breast. She quickly grabbed my hand and just simply held it, preventing me from continuing any game of foreplay. I sighed against her neck and embraced the moment of lying next to her.

"You can't let your job work you up like that," I whispered to her.

No response.

"Don't worry about Trenton. I'll listen up for him in case he gets hungry. There's still a bottle left in the fridge. You just rest up," I said as I unlocked my hand from hers, removed my arm from across her, and repositioned myself toward the bedroom door. There we lay, back-to-back, and silent.

The next morning, I was awakened by the smell of bacon. I turned over to an empty space where Natalie should have been. *I know it's not super late*, I said to myself. I looked at the alarm for confirmation on the time. It was only 6:30 a.m., and Natalie usually didn't get up until 7:00 at the earliest. As I sat on the edge of the bed, I noticed that there was no purse on the nightstand, and her keys were off the hook.

Don't trip, Marcus. There have been plenty of times when you've had to get an early jump on the day to knock out a deal, I said to myself trying to remain optimistic. She could have said goodbye, though.

After showering, I entered the kitchen to find Mia holding Trenton in her lap while fidgeting with her phone.

"Where's Grammy?" I asked.

"She went back to sleep after breakfast. She said this little guy had her up half the night."

I responded with a sad attempt at a smirk and said, "Hey, did you happen to see Natalie this morning?"

"Yep. She fixed herself tea, breastfed Trenton, and left. Why? Is something wrong?"

Pouring a cup of coffee and standing over the sink, I replied, "No—nothing's wrong. Just asking."

With coffee in hand, my mind began to wonder. *Did I do something? Was she still upset about the whole Chanel ordeal?* I then noticed Mia's mouth moving, but my mind was in such a drift that I couldn't comprehend what she was saying.

"Are you okay?" she asked. "You're acting strange this morning."

"Sorry," I replied. "I'm cool. Really, I am."

I then sat next to Mia and began playing peek-a-boo with Trenton, all the while, my mind was still parked on Natalie's strange behavior.

"Here. Go to your dad," Mia said as she extended her arms toward me. "Auntie Mia has to get dressed, but I'll be back," she continued as she made googly eyes toward a drooling Trenton.

"Morning, little fella," I said as I gently bounced him on my knee. "What do you want to do today? You wanna do something special for Mommy?"

Trenton's eyes and curled up wet mouth said it all— joy and happiness. These were two feelings that I longed for us. I just hoped that Natalie still felt the same.

Chapter 13

Natalie

I came home late, and I left early. I was a complete ball of nerves. I never was good at playing poker. The look on my face always gave away whether I had a good or bad hand. I was the same way when it came to Marcus. I would do anything for that man. Well, almost anything. I took a long hot shower when I came in last night. I used at least three different kinds of soap and scrubbed the hell out of myself with my loofah sponge. I tried to sleep but couldn't, so I went to Grammy's room, picked up my son, and held him for a little while. It was the only thing that seemed to make me feel better; it made me feel like I was still a good person, and my life still had meaning and value, and that everything would be all right. I eventually went back to bed, but I couldn't sleep, and I still felt dirty. I took another shower when I got up. I couldn't seem to get the feel of that man's hands off me and inside me. The nasty, cold tingle of his lips, the sliminess of his tongue on my neck and my nipples… it made me want to vomit just thinking about it. I got dressed quietly so I wouldn't wake Marcus. I couldn't face him, and I knew he would be able to tell that something was wrong. Then he'd keep asking me what was wrong, and the last thing I wanted to do was talk. I kept waiting for something bad to happen. Call it Karma. I also had this anxious feeling like I should do something, but I wasn't sure what.

I arrived at work extra early. I hoped that doing something productive would help take my mind off my problems. Shari wasn't in yet, so I went to the break room to fix myself a cup of coffee. As I sat there sipping it, who should walk in but Marshall Powell, the founder and CEO of the company. I rarely saw Mr. Powell. He was at an age where he was enjoying all his achievements, money, and spent quite a bit of time on the golf course or traveling with his wife. I got the feeling he didn't talk to the underlings too much anyway. He always seemed to have an air of superiority about him.

He walked in, saw me sitting at one of the small round tables that were scattered about the room, and smiled. "Hello, young lady," he said.

"Good morning, sir. How are you?"

"I'll do for an old man. What about yourself?"

"I'm fair to mid'lin, as my Grammy would say. Would you like me to fix you a cup of coffee?"

He chuckled. "I haven't heard anybody say that in years. No, I wouldn't dare interrupt you while you enjoy your cup of morning joe. I can get it myself. You're here early. It's Natalie, right?"

His comment caught me in mid-swallow, and I almost gagged. I started coughing in an attempt to hide it.

He chuckled again, "You're surprised I know your name. I always make it a priority to learn the names of the up-and-coming talent in my company. You may not know this, but I'm the reason you're here."

I raised an eyebrow.

"Oh yes. Your boyfriend, Marcus, helped my wife and me a few months back when we had a flat tire and were stranded on the side of the road. It was pouring rain that evening, and roadside assistance said they wouldn't be there anytime soon. I wanted to change the tire myself, but I couldn't. I was dealing with a nasty bout of gout in my knee and arthritis in my hands and shoulder that had me hobbling on a cane. When Marcus came along, I was feeling mighty low. It hurt my pride something awful to not be able to do a simple thing like change a tire. I'm so glad my doctors were able to help me get these aches and pains under control. My medication and a change in diet did the trick. He's a really nice fellow that there Marcus. It's a shame what happened to him. I'm glad he survived. We kept in touch, and, well, he called me a month ago and told me you were looking for a job to help out with the bills until he got back on his feet. I told him to send me your résumé, and when I saw your experience, I knew you were just the type of woman we needed here. I was right. You're doing a fine job, young lady."

"Thank you, sir." This was certainly news to me. Jackson told me he got me this job. "Marcus? He called you about hiring me?" I asked.

"Yep. Oh, darn. I wasn't supposed to tell you that. Don't tell him I told you, okay?"

"I can do that, but may I ask you a question?"

"Sure," he said while adding a ton of cream to his coffee and one pack of artificial sweetener.

"Do you know a Jackson Smith of Smith & Noble Insurance?"

The old man's face turned beet red, and he looked like he was about to explode. His lips twisted into a snarl before he answered. I was afraid I had triggered a nerve, and I was about to get a severe tongue-lashing.

"Unfortunately. That boy is rotten to the core," he said in a soft tone laced with seething contempt. "He has a bad reputation and an even worse reality. I know for a fact that son of a bitch enjoys enticing women into his bed and then recording them without their knowledge. He then uses that footage to manipulate, blackmail, and extort from his victims. He did it to my daughter, Paige, and I had to pay a hefty price to get that footage from him. If I were you, I would stay as far away from him as possible. I could have been his daddy, you know. I used to date his mother before I met my wife. She always did have a thing for rich, white men. Ooooh, Felicia was some kind of mad when I ended things. Maybe if I had been his father, he would have turned out to be a better human being." He slammed his coffee cup down on the counter, spilling a little of it.

I couldn't believe what I was hearing. The man I trusted with everything I held dear was really a monster. Jackson was hell-bent on ruining Marcus, and I gave him all the ammunition he needed to do it. I thought Jackson was my friend. I tried to hold it together, but I couldn't. I exploded into a fountain of tears.

"Why are you . . . look at me," softly ordered Mr. Powell.

I looked up at the old man with pleading eyes. I knew he could see right through me, so there was no need to hide the anguish I was feeling.

"I know that look; it's the same one my daughter gave me when she came to me to help her get that tape. Pull yourself together, Natalie." He grabbed a handful of napkins and walked them over to me. Then he went to the break room door and locked it. "That's so we won't have any interruptions. Now, you tell me everything. Don't leave out a single detail, and let's see how we can get you out of this mess."

I dried my eyes, blew my nose, and did as I was told. There was just something about Marshall Powell that said I could trust him.

Chapter 14

Marcus

The overcast clouds that painted the sky was a wonderful work of art that was highlighted by a wide gamut of pastel colors in full illumination. Anytime I need a reminder that God is real, I always looked toward the sky. It showed me that there was a world beyond my own. It often made me feel as if there is something more, something unreachable in a sense. The flow in which the clouds moved—steady, delicate, simple—were picture-perfect frames of how I envisioned my life would be, could be. However, the subtleness I longed for in Natalie and my courtship was once again being threatened.

After Mia left, Trenton and I decided to go for a stroll, and I learned that I don't need a cane if I'm pushing a stroller. We grabbed some sweet treats during our splendid father-son time; he had a bottle, and I ate a Twix. I was exhausted from making every funny face humanly possible to entertain this little boy, and he still wanted to be amused. He wasn't as enchanted by the sky as I was, so I had to incorporate a little sing-along-song to accompany the sightseeing.

Often my mind would drift back to Natalie as I continued to try to solve the complex puzzle of the relationship we shared. At times, especially last night, it seemed as if I were always trying to find a missing piece or two. As I've mentioned before, complicated is something that I tended to refrain from. At times, there is something simply organic and beautiful about our relationship. Then, there are the times when there tends to be this swirling dark cloud of doubt and untrustworthiness.

The cloudy sky had a slight breeze to accompany it, which caused Trenton to bury his little body deeper into the comfort of my chest. My attention was once again directed toward the awkward behavior of Natalie. Trust was something that has taken me some time to regain, and I was beginning to feel as if I no longer trusted Natalie. My internal triggers were going off, and I knew whatever she was hiding wouldn't be something that I could just sweep under the rug. Trenton and I decided to make a trip to Natalie's place of work and confront the situation head-on. I did not intend to have any type of dispute in front of her coworkers; I was too professional to do anything like that. My plan was just to pop up and surprise her with an impromptu lunch date with the three of us.

When I arrived at her office, I got that feeling again. That feeling that will never escape me: comfort, natural, and passion. This was the feeling I maintained when I was working on being the best business professional in my peer group. There was just something about office buildings that made my blood pump success.

I buzzed the ringer to alert the front desk that Trenton and I were in the lobby.

A woman rounded the corner and said, "May I help you?" She was friendly with a slight accent.

"Yes. I'm Marcus Colbert. I'm a friend—I mean, I'm Natalie Tellis' fiancé."

"Oh! Sure thing. I'll tell Ms. Tellis you're here. Hold tight. I'm her assistant, Shari." She disappeared as quickly as she came.

Trenton didn't like to be in his stroller if it wasn't moving, and he began to let the world know that he was in the building. I picked him up but my attempts at trying to calm him down were wearing thin. I was finally able to quiet him by humming a light tune. We waited patiently. Well, I waited patiently for another five minutes or so before Natalie arrived.

"Hi. What are you doing here, Marcus?" Natalie asked with a puzzled look on her face.

With Trenton now drooling and reacting to the voice of his mother, I replied, "We just wanted to come and surprise you with a little lunch. Too busy?"

She was hesitant with her reply. Honestly, it kind of hurt my feelings. She didn't look happy to see me or Trenton. Now, I knew something wasn't right with her. She was wearing guilt like it was one of her favorite pieces of clothing. "I just wish you would have called beforehand—that's all."

Still coddling Trenton close to my chest, I said, "Well, I was hoping we could also discuss some other things as well."

"Marcus, this couldn't wait until I came home?" she asked with a slight irritation in her tone. After realizing what she'd said and my reaction, she continued, "I didn't mean it like that." She reached for my hand as she continued, "I don't want to seem ungrateful. I truly love that you and my little man want to spend your afternoon with me, but I—"

"Here is the man himself, Mr. Marcus Colbert. You know, the ol' lady is still showing her appreciation for you taking care of that little flat we had," Mr. Powell said as he walked into the lobby, and he shot a playful wink my way. "This must be the little fella. Why, aren't you handsome. What's your name, son?"

"Say, my name is Trenton," I replied.

"What brings y'all out this way?" he asked.

"Well, we were hoping to take this lovely lady here out for a quick bite, but it seems as if she's too occupied right now with something, so I think we're gonna just lunch alone today."

Mr. Powell glimpsed Natalie's way for a quick sec before focusing his attention back toward me. "Oh, it's all my fault, Marcus. You know what? I didn't tell her about this large account one of our key producers had dropped the ball on. I need her expertise in putting some things together. Being the businessman that you are, I'm sure you can understand, right?"

"I understand." I'll admit, Mr. Powell soothed my suspicions. Maybe this was all just a misunderstanding. I then began to feel guilty for even thinking Natalie was up to something. Therefore, my initial sentiments were confirmed. Work was creating that uncomfortable wedge between Natalie and me. Trenton and I said our good-byes, and we left.

Chapter 15

Natalie

It's an unnerving thing to put your life in the hands of someone else. Especially, someone that you don't know very well. Mr. Powell seemed like a trustworthy man, but right about now, it's hard for me to trust anyone outside of my family. He asked me not to do anything in regards to Jackson and give him a few days to figure out the best way to get him to leave me alone for good. I'm pretty sure I don't have a few days. That vulture is going to circle around again soon, but I planned to do as I was told. I was also instructed not to be alone with him under any circumstances. That part was easy. I had no desire to be in the same vicinity as that man. Now, lying to Marcus and keeping my composure while doing it is another thing. I knew that he knew something was wrong. I never come in late without calling, and I left early to avoid any questions I wasn't prepared to answer. I had to get my story straight before I went home. If I didn't, I'd blurt out the truth, and that wasn't good for anyone right about now. Marcus was going through a lot, and I didn't want to add to the stress.

There was a feeling in the pit of my stomach that I knew was a result of the loathing I felt for a man I once thought was my friend. It felt like indigestion, bubble guts, and menstrual cramps all rolled up into one. I wanted to call Jackson and give him a piece of my mind, and I wanted to egg his prized luxury vehicle. I wanted to pee in his cornflakes! This was the first time I had come face-to-face with that kind of evil and manipulation. I wondered how much of anything he had told me over the past few years were lies and how much was the truth. I wanted to go home and gather all the things he'd bought my son and me, take them to his house, and set them on fire in his front yard.

I tried to sit at my desk and focus on my work. Unfortunately, Jackson and this horrific predicament I'm in kept coming to the forefront of my thoughts. I looked out the window and stared at the beautiful blue sky. On a day like this, I should be able to enjoy the nice weather and reflect on how great my life is. I'm a new mother, with a job I enjoy, and a man I love, but I have to have some asshole trying to blackmail me into letting him play in my . . . Damn! Why me? This is too much! I need a drink, a valium, and a Xanax.

I heard my phone vibrate, and when I realized it was Jackson, I felt the bile rise in my throat. Thankfully, I didn't vomit. He sent a text. HELLO, BEAUTIFUL. LET'S PICK UP WHERE WE LEFT OFF. TONIGHT, MY PLACE, AT 9:00 P.M. I MADE SURE THAT IT WON'T HAPPEN AGAIN.

God had mercy on me last night, after all that planning and plotting to do evil; that offspring of Freddy Kruger and Carrie couldn't perform. His little soldier refused to salute long enough to finish what he tried to start. He approached me in an attempt to enter my sacred place, and he went limp as a noodle. But that didn't stop him from putting his hands and mouth anywhere he wanted. I guess he's gotten some Viagra, smoked some weed, or drank some Mad Dog 20/20, but I don't care, and I'm not going to find out if he is in working order or not. I am going to go home to my family and make them dinner. I put a block on his phone calls but not the texts in case he sent something I could use against him. I needed to clear my head. After our break room chat, Mr. Powell told me I could take the rest of the day off, but I decided to stay. I didn't want to get behind and allow the other candidates to outshine me. I wanted a job at this company, and I wanted one of the high-paying ones, too. Those would go to the candidates who outperformed everyone else, which means the ones who helped to retain and bring in the most business. My staying worked in my favor since Marcus decided to drop by unannounced. Quitting time was near and I figured a couple of hours in the gym would help with the anxiety I was feeling.

As I headed to the garage, I got a phone call from Mia, and I sent her to voicemail. There was no way I could deal with her teenage drama today. Things between Mia and me had been somewhat estranged for the past few months. While I was in the hospital recuperating, she borrowed my car without permission. She also borrowed my home. I'm positive the only reason she didn't have her house parties at Marcus's place was because she didn't know the security code to deactivate his alarm. That little heifer took both our keys when we were in the hospital fighting for our lives, and she probably would have gotten away with it if my apartment manager hadn't called me on one of my good days, when I wasn't in excruciating pain and doped up, to ask me why teenyboppers were coming in and out of my place all times of the day and night. I knew immediately who was behind it, and I instructed him to change the locks the next day. I then called Ms. Mia. She tried to lie and tell me she was at the library studying. I let her know I knew exactly where she was and told her she had thirty minutes to get everyone out of my place before I called the cops and an hour to bring me my keys. She also had better leave my place exactly as she found it. There was no way I was coming home to a nasty apartment, after all I had been through.

When Mia brought me my keys, she came in with those wide, puppy dog, watery eyes that seemed to work on her parents and Marcus, but she got absolutely no sympathy from me. The only grace I granted her was if she stayed out of trouble, I wouldn't tell any of them. So far, she seemed to have upheld her end of the bargain. Once I was released and able to inspect my car, I realized that it had several dings on it, but no major damage. My apartment reeked of weed, but at least she cleaned up. Although I'm not pleased with her behavior, I still miss her. Mia is smart, funny, and kind but a little mischievous and obviously naive about boys. She had become the little sister I always wanted, but when she betrayed my trust, I had to put some distance between us. I guess that's a normal defense mechanism. I had forgiven her, but something deep inside me wouldn't let me allow the closeness we once had. Therefore, when she sent me a text a couple of days ago, stating that she was in trouble and needed to talk as we once did, I told her to contact Marcus. As her brother, he's obligated to deal with her teenage hormonal issues, and I wasn't. It seemed as if she took my advice when I saw her asleep on the couch when I came in last night. Maybe Marcus would tell me what they talked about tonight at dinner. I wondered if she was still messing with grown men. I suggested to Marcus that he put a tracker on her phone, but he said since she was eighteen and legally grown, he felt doing so was an invasion of her privacy. I also informed him that as long as he was helping to pay her bills, in my opinion, he had every right to keep up with her whereabouts. He bought the phone. I wanted to tell him so bad what she had done. I knew he would put a tracker on her phone then, but a promise was a promise.

I was anxious to get to the gym, and I hoped the punching bag was open, as I was going to pretend that it was Jackson's face. Getting my body back was one of my postpregnancy goals, and I wanted to lose at least forty pounds and this gut. Putting in long hours at work had prevented me from getting there like I needed to, so I hadn't made much progress. Yep. I would go work out, then head to the store for the groceries I needed to make my man's favorite meal. Jackson wasn't going to win. I was going to keep my family safe and intact at all costs. You could put that on everything.

Chapter 16

Marcus

It had been about a week since Natalie and I began experiencing this awkward space between us, emotionally and physically. Our loved ones must have sensed the tension as they blessed us with a little mommy-and-daddy vacation. I'll admit the first night was one to forget.

Things started badly from the jump, almost to the point where I wanted to plead with my mom and Grammy to cancel whatever they had for us. It all started when I simply requested that Natalie put the toothpaste back in the holder before leaving the bathroom.

"Oh, now you got shit to say. Ain't heard much from you in days, and you want to discuss some damn tooth-paste."

I tried to hold my tongue, but the tone in her voice irked me to the point where I responded with, "If I didn't have to walk around here like Sherlock Holmes all the damn time trying to figure out why my lady has been acting like a stranger in the night, maybe the topic of conversation wouldn't be some fucking toothpaste."

I'll admit it had felt good to get that off of my chest. She responded by forcefully shoving the toothpaste upside-down in the holder. I bore down on my teeth tight like a child that didn't want their teeth brushed.

Then, I looked in the mirror and said, "Lord, I don't think you are too fond of me. Out of *all* the women in the world to bless me with, you bless me with pure

craziness." It didn't stop there. Once I gathered myself
and walked back into the bedroom, I saw Natalie
rearranging my overnight bag that I had spent the last
thirty minutes strategically organizing. The internal bomb
had already been ticking.

"What are you doing?" I asked with some edge in my
tone.

"I'm helping you out, thank you very much."

Leaning heavily on my cane, I reached to grab my
bag and replied, "I don't need your help with this. I think
I'm old enough to pack my own damn bag."

Rolling her eyes and willingly allowing me to take
back possession of my bag, she replied, "Fine. Have it
your way."

"Fine. I am," I mumbled to myself as I stared into
my rearranged bag. I saw that everything was perfectly
aligned, and I even had extra space to add more things if
I needed to. I hated the fact that she had packed my bag
better than I had, but I wouldn't dare give her the
satisfaction. So, I shuffled things around aggressively in
my bag in an attempt to show her who was boss. I ended
up with a mess of a job, but at least I still felt in control
of my balls.

After Natalie and I reluctantly said our goodbyes to
baby Trenton, we put all our things in the trunk of the
car and prepped to hit the road toward Gatlinburg,
Tennessee. No more than five minutes into the ride, we
were at it again. I can't even remember what it was over,
but whatever it was, I'm sure it was petty. I was channel
surfing the satellite radio when I heard Natalie say to
herself, "Jeez, I hate this song." No sooner than she
made that statement, I put the volume on twenty and

even pretended like I knew the lyrics. Truth be told, I hated that damn song too, but not today.

It was starting to get dark when we arrived in Gatlinburg. I was concentrating extra hard as I maneuvered through the winding maze of a mountain to get to our cabin. "Be careful, babe," escaped from the lips of the madwoman sitting on the passenger-side. When she said it, I took a quick glimpse at her. The guilt of my pettiness began to show on my face and hers, too. However, neither of us wanted to take that first step in being the adult in the situation. We sat in silence, both watching the road as I cautiously drove.

The cabin was beautiful, the scenery, setting, and sexiness of the cabin were one for the record books. "Damn, who could have imagined Grammy knew how to get her sexy on!" I said in an apologetic tone. We could have missed out on this arguing over stupid stuff.

After checking out the cabin and unpacking our bags, we uncorked the bottle of Merlot that was sitting on the kitchen island with a red bow on it. We sat down on a massive brown leather couch, turned on the television and landed on a show called *Black Love*. It must have been a marathon because it was four hours later and two bottles of wine emptied before we began to open up.

"Damn, I guess we aren't the only ones who have crazy relationships," I said with my arm now wrapped around Natalie's shoulder.

She snuggled closer to me. As she looked into my eyes, I could sense that there was something she wanted to say to me. However, I didn't allow her to. I placed my index finger to her lips and told her, "No words right now." I don't know if it was the wine or watching those other couples tell their struggle stories and making it through, but whatever it was, we most definitely got our flow back on that couch. It was amazing, emotional, and intense; the perfect combination. After our intensity expired, we lay there totally drained.

Natalie eventually sat up and said, "I'm getting some water—want some?" I playfully smacked her on her backside and said, "You know what I want." She blushed and dressed her face with the seductive look I loved and replied, "I'm game for round three, or is it four? I lost count." We both laughed.

When she left, I heard her phone buzzing by the couch. I had forgotten that we didn't let my mom or Grammy know that we had made it. I called out to her to let her know, but she didn't hear me. It started to buzz again, so I reached for it. After adjusting my eyes to the light, I noticed that there was a text that read, YOU KNOW YOU WANT THIS. NOW STOP PLAYING AND COME SEE BIG DADDY. I'M FEENIN FOR YOU AND MY PATIENCE IS RUNNING OUT.

Chapter 17

Natalie

I opened the refrigerator and grabbed two bottles of water. It felt good to have some alone time with Marcus. No work, no Trenton, no Grammy, no Mia, and best of all, no Jackson. I closed the door, turned around and almost dropped both bottles as I came to an abrupt stop to avoid a head-on collision with an angry-looking Marcus. His face looked entirely different from less than five minutes ago when he playfully hit me on my naked behind. Now, here we were, both naked in the kitchen of this gorgeous cabin, surrounded by stainless steel appliances that reflected the glow of the pale moonlight seeping through several windows scattered around the room. Even with this entire splendor, one of us looked like we were about to explode.

"Did you fuck Jackson?"

"What? No. What would make you ask that?"

"This!" he said as he shoved my phone an inch from my face as if I could read it in such close proximity.

I took the phone from him. "What in the world . . ." my voice trailed off as I read the message.

"I'm tired of this shit, Natalie. I told you to cut off all contact with him months ago. You have five seconds to explain this message—and no lies."

"Okay. No lies. Come have a seat." I grabbed him by the hand to lead him to the table, but he snatched it away.

"You're stalling, Natalie. I want answers, and I want answers NOW!"

My feet felt cold on the floor, and my nipples began to harden from the chill in the air. I wondered if it was the temperature in the room or Marcus' disposition that made me want to put on a sweater. Yet, I couldn't walk away. I had to face this man and tell him what he wanted to know. I took a deep breath, and a series of words began to roll off my tongue a mile a minute. I began telling him the details of what had transpired between us.

Marcus' face was blank. He didn't say a word, and I couldn't read him. His face held no indication of what he might have been thinking. He walked away. I just stood there. Two minutes later, he made his way back to me with a blanket, genitals slanging along the way.

"You look cold," he said and wrapped it around my shoulders.

We both walked to the table and had a seat. I continued, "Jackson tried to sleep with me, but his plan backfired, and now he's trying to blackmail me so he can try a second time. I didn't sleep with him, I swear. He told me he'd ruin both our lives if I didn't, and the reason I didn't tell you is that I thought I could handle it. Mr. Powell said he would help me, too. It turns out Jackson slept with his daughter, recorded it, and blackmailed her. From my understanding, he's done that to several women. I've never had intercourse with Jackson, but for some reason, he has this incessant need to prove he's better than you by having everything you have and more. That's the truth. I swear it's the truth. Please believe me, baby. Please."

Marcus sat in silence for about three minutes and said softly, "You should have come to me, Natalie. I'm your man. It's my job to protect you."

"I didn't want to worry you. And Jackson said he would ruin our lives. He said he would put my brother and Manny in jail. He said he would get me fired from my job, and you know how much we need the money right now. He made me believe he got me that job. I had no idea it was you. He also said you would never believe me, and I believed him. We've come so far. I couldn't take a chance on losing you. You and Trenton mean everything to me. I love you, Marcus."

"I love you too, Natalie, but Jackson is the devil, and you don't negotiate with the devil. You will lose every time. Did you agree to meet him tonight?"

"No. Mr. Powell told me to ignore all his messages, but he keeps texting me, though."

"You should have done that in the beginning. You know you could have told me."

I wondered how many times he was going to say that. I looked down at my hands. "Jackson sent flowers to my job with an anonymous invitation to meet him at a hotel. I assumed they were from you. I thought you were being romantic. Once I was in the room, I didn't know how to get out of it. I mean I was in a hotel room in sexy lingerie. You had already been through so much. I thought I could handle it."

"Are you sure that's all? There wasn't some small part of you that was enjoying having a man who could still do all the things a man could do in your life, and it didn't excite you at all? Maybe Jackson was your backup plan."

"Never! Marcus, from the day I met you, all I wanted was you. How dare you accuse me of wanting someone else! You've pursued other women the majority of the time I've known you—when we were together, and when we were not together."

"You're right. That was a low blow. I've been so busy feeling sorry for myself, I forget that my woman needs me. I found that letter he wrote to you, the one where he poured out his heart to you and asked you to leave me. He even had the nerve to say he wished I had died during the shooting. I can't believe I once thought that fool was my friend."

Where did he find that letter? I didn't even know where it was. "Oh, I lit into his ass after he sent that. I told him we would never be together, and he had better not ever say any bullshit like that again. He apologized immediately."

Marcus came over and kissed me on my forehead. Then, he gathered me into his arms and gave me a warm hug. "I'm sorry, Natalie. Don't worry your pretty little head about it. Jackson is my problem now. I'll handle him. Keep ignoring him until I tell you otherwise."

I didn't like the sound of his voice. It sounded evil and sinister. Not at all like the Marcus I knew and loved. "What are you going to do?" I asked.

"Simple. Show him that you don't mess with Marcus Colbert or anything that belongs to me. You do belong to me, right?"

"Of course, I do," I said as I stood and seductively unwrapped the blanket from around my shoulders and let it fall to the floor. My nipples were rock hard and pointing directly at him. Marcus' eyes widened.

"Do you belong to me?" I asked.

Marcus took a step toward me and licked his lips. "I do. I'm completely and totally yours." His once limp member began to respond to the magnetism between us. He took one hand and began to fondle my left breast. "From now on, I promise that you will have no reason to go to any man for any reason . . . love, support, attention, money—nothing. I'll be everything you need, and more."

Marcus then bent down and took my breast in his mouth. I closed my eyes and enjoyed the warmth of his mouth and tongue on my cold, hard areola. It sent a shiver through my body that caused me to shudder. Then, I felt my body being lifted from the floor and carried to the master bedroom of the cabin. There, my man proceeded to make love to me again, but it didn't feel the same as before. It felt like he was trying to establish his territory instead of demonstrating his affection for me. If I had to put it in layman's terms, I would say he was like a dog pissing on a hydrant . . . and *I* was the hydrant.

Chapter 18

Marcus

This thing called love can be one of the most difficult journeys a man may travel in a lifetime. There's beauty underneath the ugliness, joy in the midst of the pain, and relief during times of stress. I guess that's where the phrase "crazy in love" stems from because you got to be one crazy motherfucker to voluntarily put yourself through all the bullshit that's associated with it.

Not too long after Natalie and I had another "sweat session," I stepped away to the outside balcony. The view was beyond amazing, the beautiful balance of all the greens in addition to the heightened level we were on, made it seem as if I were on the stairway to heaven. God really outdid himself when he blessed us with one of the loveliest and important births of Mother Earth—the tree.

Unbeknownst to Natalie, I always keep a hidden stash of cigarettes somewhere near for times such as this. My life, my vice. As the taste of menthol satisfied my nightly fix, I sat deep in thought about this whole Jackson and Natalie ordeal. None of it seemed real to me. I've always joked and teased Natalie about all the unrealistic, over-the-top, and buffoonery-type movies and television shows she loved to watch, but here we were, caught right up in the rapture of all the fuckery in real life. This is our movie, and it's time to cut out one of its cast members.

"Marcus, are you out here?" a raspy-voiced Natalie whispered as she turned on one of the balcony lights.

"Yes. I'm out here," I said as I hurriedly smashed my half-smoked cigarette inside a mosquito repellant candle.

The wood creaked as Natalie headed in my direction.

"Ma'am, you better hit that light before you come this way. You're messing up the ambiance I got going on."

Natalie sat by my side and playfully nudged me in my rib cage and replied, "Is that right, mister? I'm *all* the ambiance you need."

She gently slid one of her legs toward my groin, allowing me to get a subtle glimpse of the sexiness of her upper thigh as her nightgown began to roll up.
"Is that so?" I replied. "So, what type of ambiance you trying to create right now?" I continued as I firmly grabbed the back of her leg, causing her to submit fully to sitting atop of me, face-to-face.

"I'm not stupid, Marcus, I know you been out here smoking," she said as she began to use her investigative nose to sniff me up and down, around my neck and chest.

I leaned forward to kiss her lips, but she playfully rejected my offer. "I don't want any of that secondhand smoke from your lips," she joked.

"Girl, you better get all of this loving I got to offer," I replied, returning the playful nature.

"Seriously though, why are you out here smoking? I thought you were done with that."

"I am. I mean, I was." She rolled from atop me and sat by my side. "It's like this, every now and then, I still like to have a smoke. It eases me in some ways. I mean, we've been through so much in a short span that I needed something, and this just so happens to be it."

"But you know how I feel about that. Also, did you forget you only have one full lung now? Why would you risk damaging it?"

"I'll make a deal with you. If you promise to be open with me from here on out about everything—and I do mean everything—I'll try my best not to smoke again." She nudged me once more. "Seriously, if you do that for me, I'll do this for you."

"It's that simple?" she asked.

"Anything can be simple. We, as humans, just make life difficult as fuck."

She rested her head on my shoulder and tucked her arms inside my robe as the night air created a nice chill. "I love you, Marcus." She hugged me tightly inside the warmth of my robe and continued, "I really love you. I'll do almost anything for you."

"*Almost?* I'm curious now. What wouldn't you do?" I asked.

"I don't know off-hand. But I know the list is short."

"What about lie for me?" I asked.

"Of course."

"Would you steal for me?"

"If I needed to." She turned her head toward me, and I continued.

"I got one. What about a threesome?"

She pinched one of my nipples and replied, "You so nasty."

"Well, would you?"

"Sorry, mister, I can't do that one. I'm a one-person lover."

"I thought you said anything."

"I said *almost* anything."

"I was just teasing anyway. I can't handle or need any more women in my life." I kissed the top of her head. Natalie had been wearing her hair natural since the baby, and I loved the smell of the products she used.

"So, let me flip the question. What wouldn't you do for me?" she asked.

"At this point, I probably would do just about anything for you as well."

"I need more, mister. Let me ask you some 'would-you' questions." She raised up and began to quiz me. "Would you go a whole week and watch my television shows with me without complaining?"

"I ain't gonna lie; it would be tough, but I'd do it."

"Would you die for me?"

"That's so cliché," I replied.

"Wait. Your questions were soooo cliché. Don't be trying to avoid the question. Either you would, or you wouldn't. My feelings won't be hurt."

"I guess it would depend on the situation."

"Fair enough. I got another one. Would you kill for me?"

"Why you asking all these ID Channel-type questions? You got something you need to tell me?" I replied in a joking tone.

She laughed and said, "I'm just asking." She then had more of a serious tone and asked, "Will you ever forgive me for all that I've put you through?"

That was the million-dollar question. "Natalie, to be fair, I have no choice but to forgive you. I've caused my fair share of hurt toward you as well. The question should be, can I ever forgive *myself* for not seeing the beauty within you earlier? How about we forgive each other?"

She nodded in agreement and smiled that perfect smile of hers. She then sat back atop me, wrapped her arms around my neck, and whispered in my ear, "Now, about that threesome minus one . . ."

We both shared a laugh and started another sweat session on a wooden swing in the company of the beautiful blanket of greenery in the mountains. I'm obviously healthier than I thought I was.

Chapter 19

Natalie

As much as I was enjoying the personal attention from Marcus, I couldn't help worrying. I just told him that his ex-best friend was trying to blackmail his fiancée into having sex with him in exchange for silence, and Marcus was as cool as a cucumber. All he seemed to want to do was ravage me. I know him well enough to know that he's up to something. While he pleases me, a plan for revenge is being concocted in that handsome head of his. The part that scares me is that I have no idea what it is. He hasn't even mentioned Jackson's name since I confessed to him about how I even gave Jackson ammunition to blackmail me. After reading his texts, Marcus told me to cut off my phone. I offered to block Jackson's texts too, but Marcus said we might need future texts as evidence. Cutting off my phone would allow us to enjoy our time together now and view whatever that sicko had to say later.

I was lying across the bed void of all clothing as he massaged every inch of me with warm oil, and he gently placed kisses in my most sensitive spots as he worked. His hands skillfully kneaded my stress-filled flesh, forcing it to release the toxic bodily reaction to days of unhappiness and guilt. He was quiet as he moved along the folds of my body. Almost too quiet. I've only seen Marcus like this just one time before, and that was with my brother and Manny. I knew he was cooking up something to get revenge after he found out that they assaulted him, and I begged him to drop it. I begged him not to hurt my brother and best friend or make me take sides. Jessie is my little brother. I'm sworn to protect him, but when it comes to Jackson, I have no allegiance to him or deep concern for his well-being. I used to, though. But that was before I discovered that he was a sexual predator, and I'm glad I told Marcus. This was too much of a burden to bear on my own. Yet, what did my man have up his sleeve? I planned to ask him but not until after we left Gatlinburg. I'm going to get every ounce of attention out of this love train before it pulls back into the station called home.

I let out a soft sigh as Marcus planted another kiss on my body. I could definitely see why Lisa began drinking herself into a stupor after letting him go, and why Chanel was willing to betray her best friend to have him. This man definitely knew how to please a woman, and if it's a woman he holds a deep affection for, his passion for her is on a whole 'nother level. I let out another sigh as he softly placed kisses within the folds of a place that made my insides warmer than the oil he was using to rub me down. Nothing mattered at that moment but our love. If I could make time stand still, I would.

Unfortunately, we had to go home soon.

Chapter 20

Marcus

"Can you handle that? If so, consider it done." Those were the last words I spoke into the phone before Natalie walked back inside the room. I immediately said my goodbyes and proceeded to focus my attention on her.

"Nervous?" I asked.

"A little, but I'm confident," Natalie replied. Natalie was taking her test for her producer's license today. She was wrapping up her Junior Management Trainee program at Powell, Johnson, and Haynes, and she wanted to be sure that she had all the necessary credentials afterward to be in a great position to advance her career if the opportunity presented itself.

Neither of us was able to get much sleep the night before as I drilled and quizzed her to be sure that she knew the material inside and out. "You want to go over it one more time?" I asked.

She shook her head. "I don't want to overthink things. I think I'm good to go."

With a smirk on my face and a playful tone, I replied, "Well, look at you all confident and stuff."

She allowed a smile to break through her nervousness. Then she sighed and said, "I can't help but to be confident with you in my corner." I will admit that it felt good to hear her say that.

About two weeks had passed since she revealed to me at the cabin the inner workings and evildoings of

Jackson. Since that time, Jackson sent several text messages. They started out asking Natalie to meet him, but when she didn't respond, they turned into name-calling and threats. The last one came yesterday, and it simply said, "NO ONE IGNORES JACKSON SMITH. YOU'RE GOING TO REGRET THIS."

"Well, I got some good news to share as well," I said.

"Really? What is it?"

"I got a start date to return to work. I'll be back in full swing in about four weeks."

"That's awesome, Marcus," she said with glee. "Is that who you were talking to when I walked in?"

"Yes," I lied.

"I just knew things were going to turn around for good." Natalie then looked back at me as she headed toward the bedroom door to get her things. "Good news looks good on us, Marcus."

When I knew that Natalie had left the condo, I called my mom to check on Trenton. She agreed to keep him last night so Natalie could study in peace. Afterward, I immediately called Manny back to finalize some details of our proposed plan to take Jackson out once and for all. I had bumped into Manny at the gas station a week ago. We had a real man-to-man conversation about everything. It took every bone in my body to check my ego at the door and let what happened between Manny and me pass for the moment, but I did. I looked at the bigger picture, which was Jackson. I knew Manny had a sweet spot for money, and he didn't like anything harmful to come Natalie's way, so he was perfect for helping me execute my plan to get revenge on Jackson.

"Are you sure Natalie doesn't know what's going on?" he asked.

"She doesn't have a clue, I can assure you of that," I replied.

"Well, I had a friend of mine check on a few things, and it looks like this brother is deeply rooted in some wild shit. He even sold a little coke." Manny chuckled and continued, "My guy said it's gonna cost you, but he can get it done."

"Listen, money is not an issue; I just don't want any loose ends lingering afterward." I never figured Jackson as a drug dealer, but I knew he used a little coke every now and then.

Manny allowed some silence to cut through the conversation before he replied, "I'm good on my end. You just make sure you do the same on yours."

"I can assure you, everything will go as planned."

Chapter 21

Natalie

"Natalie, he tried to rape me!" screamed Mia.

"Mia, baby, calm down. Who tried to rape you?"

"I can't tell you."

This girl knew how to work a nerve, but I had come to love her like my own sibling, and she was going to tell me everything whether she liked it or not. "What? Someone tried to force themselves on you, and you can't tell me?"

"First, you have to promise that you won't tell Marcus."

I knew Mia was upset and to the point of tears, but I wasn't going to lie to her. "I'm not going to promise you that. He's your brother, and that's absurd. If someone tried to hurt you, he deserves to know."

"No, you can't tell anyone. I was so stupid," she whined.

"Mia, you are not stupid. No man has the right to take advantage of you. Just tell me what the hell is going on, and then I'll decide who needs to know what. It's the family's job to protect you, and I can't do that if I don't know where the threat is."

She took a deep breath. "Well, okay. I went over to his house to return his car. Since you and Marcus wouldn't let me use your cars, and he had more than one, I took him up on his offer to borrow one. He let me use it when I asked. I asked him what I owed him, and he told me we would work something out later. He didn't even make me put gas in it, and it had a full tank every time I got it. I mean, I've known him for most of my life. I never thought he would try to hurt me. To-night, when I tried to return the car, he told me it was time to pay what I owe. He kissed me. I kissed him back at first, but when he tried to take it further, I said, 'No.' He tried to have sex with me, and I mean, he's fine, but he's like Marcus' age, so he's like an old man to me. I know when I'm in over my head, and when I told him I wasn't interested, he threw me on the couch, grabbed my breasts, and starting kissing me. I told him to-to-to-to-stop. He didn't. I started screaming, and that's when he told me to shut up, or he'd kill my entire family. I kept screaming. He put his hands in my pants, and I asked him not to do this, that my parents would be so mad. I guess the thought of Momma and Daddy did something to him. He stopped, got off of me, and told me to get out. I ran like hell to a friend's house who lived close by. I'm with Tasha now, headed home."

"Mia, who is 'him'? Tell me who this bastard is," I ordered.

She burst into tears and sobbed before blurting out. "It was Jackson. Jackson tried to rape me; he was like family to me. I never thought he would hurt me."

My body flushed hot with anger. I saw red all around me. Evidently, the heat within my body dried up all the saliva in my mouth because suddenly, I was thirstier than I had ever been.

"Natalie? Natalie, say something. Are you there?" Mia squealed.

That son of a bitch had to die. Messing with women my age was one thing, but Mia was only eighteen.

"I'm here. Are you OK? Did he hurt you?"

"No. I'm all right, just a little shaken. I've never seen that side of him before. He's always been so kind and concerned."

"That's what predators do, Mia. They earn your trust—then attack. Go home and get some rest. I'll call you back. No worries, I got this. Stay away from Jackson. Don't do anything."

"Yes, ma'am. Natalie, what are you going to do?"

I didn't want to upset her more so I said as calmly and sweetly as I could, "Sweetheart, don't worry about me. I'm going to do what I said and keep you safe. I promise you that Jackson will never hurt another woman again."

I had to tell Marcus. This was too important to keep from him, but it needed a face-to-face conversation. I can't remember how I got home; the drive is an absolute blur, but I got home only to find Marcus standing in the living room wearing a suit. Both his parents were there, and so was Grammy. She was holding Trenton, and Pepper was yapping at her feet wearing a black-and-white doggie tux. Even my brother and his girlfriend were there. I hadn't seen Jessie in months. All his hard work had paid off, and he was a chiseled mass of muscles. I knew if I hugged him, it would feel like hugging steel. Manny, Shari and my godmother, Dr. Adina Frank was there, too. It was good to see everybody, but I was totally confused. It wasn't my birthday, and everyone I loved was in the room, so I knew no one had died. Did some other tragedy occur that I wasn't aware of?

"Welcome home, Natalie," Marcus said.

"Hey, everybody," I said, addressing everyone in the room as I scanned it. "What's going on?"

"I know I already asked you, but I wanted to do this decent and in order." Marcus came and stood in front of me and then, stooped down to one knee. He looked so handsome in the navy blue suit he was wearing. He even wore the pink tie and matching handkerchief I bought him for Christmas. "Natalie, I know we've had our issues, but these last few months and a near-death experience have shown me that life is nothing without someone wonderful to share it with. You are a smart and beautiful woman with a kind heart. You have loved me unconditionally, even when I didn't deserve it, and you have given me the greatest gift I ever had, our son." As if on cue, Trenton started babbling in the background and reaching for me. "I want to have more amazing moments with you. I want to have more children with you, and I want to spend the rest of our lives loving each other as husband and wife."

Then Marcus reached into his breast pocket and pulled out a black velvet box. He opened it, and sitting inside a satin cushion was a large diamond surrounded by sparkling blue sapphires. It was beautiful! This moment was beautiful.

"Natalie Tellis, will you do me the honor of being my wife?" He took the ring out of the box and slid it on my finger.

All the anger I felt when I walked through the door was replaced by joy. Marcus was beaming at me, and I knew he meant every word he said. Tears streamed from my eyes as I nodded my head profusely. "Yes, baby. Yes, I'll marry you!" I screamed. I grabbed him and hugged him as tightly as I could while thinking, *How are my dreams coming true in the middle of a nightmare?*

How the hell was I going to tell him about Jackson now? Also, there was no way I was going to get to the bedroom to get my gun and leave without anybody noticing. I guess he gets to breathe God's precious air for one more day. But as far as I was concerned, Jackson's days were numbered.

Chapter 22

Marcus

I must say that it felt good to be surrounded by loved ones at such a time. When I first asked Natalie to marry me, it was like the ending of a long-ass novel. Not that our story was coming to an end, but it's time for a new story with more chapters, different subplots, and fresh characters. This is an accomplishment for us. Through all the challenges, and there were a lot of them, it finally feels like my life—our life—is moving in a direction that doesn't seem foggy. No longer were we traveling into the land of the unknown.

To see my friends and family comingling with Natalie's, and it wasn't due to a tragedy or drama, was refreshing. We were together out of love. The only person missing from the special occasion was Mia. I had been trying to contact her all day. I finally reached her, and she told me that I should have contacted her earlier because she had plans. I wondered what those plans were. When I asked, she avoided the question. I realized that she has her own life to live, so I'm trying to give her the space she needs, but I will always be her protector. I guess that's why Jessie and I have gotten closer. I understand why he did what he did, and I may not ever get over it, but I've dropped the ego, and we're starting anew.

When Natalie walked in all wide-eyed, I knew the waterworks would soon follow. "I love you so much," she whispered in my ear after a long and warm embrace.

"I love you back," I said.

Shari, Natalie's assistant from work, did an extraordinary job creating the ambiance within the room. The food arrangement, décor, and music selection were just what the doctor ordered. Natalie was overjoyed when she realized that everyone had supplied her with bottles of Kisses by Rihanna and Hershey's chocolate candy kisses. It was my idea for such a spoof, but at least, it's her favorite.

"How has your day been, babe?" I asked as we snuck away from the crowd for a little one-on-one time.

Sitting on my lap with Trenton in hers, she replied,

"It's been a day. That's about all I can say."

Her facial expression said more. Over time, you tend to learn tidbits of nonverbal questions and answers from your partner. Plus, Natalie was a terrible liar.

"Work got you on edge?" I probed.

"Work is fine. I'm glad the test is over. Now, I'm waiting on the results, but that's not what's bothering me."

"So, something *is* bothering you."

Her face reddened. She tried to get up, but I pulled her back down.

"What's wrong, babe?"

She began to tear up. "All of this is so overwhelming."

"In a good way, I hope?"

"Trust me. All of *this* is very good."

I knew she wasn't telling me the whole truth, but I decided to let it go. Why kick up dirt and ruin a special time? I wanted to enjoy the moment, because there were some other things I needed to do that weren't so pleasant. After about ten minutes, everyone was calling our names to get back to the party. I guess there were more surprises on deck. I sought out Manny because we have some unfinished business to discuss.

***

The nightmares I'd been having on my road to recovery had subsided a great deal. The headaches were less frequent, and I was growing stronger with each passing day. Physical therapy was going well, and I no longer needed a cane. Since I stopped smoking, my breathing was better. All my doctors said I was making great progress.

"Who would have thought?" Manny asked.

"Thought what?"

"Who would have thought that you and I would be sitting here talking—like this?"

I nodded. "I'll admit, when I first reached out, I was kind of skeptical, but you know like I know, a man has limits."

"Especially when it comes to family," he said.

"Especially family."

"So, I talked to my guy, and he said he could get it for you for about two-fifty."

"That's all?" I asked.

"Listen, I told you I was good on my end."

I thanked Manny for arranging for me to get a gun that can't be traced. He then called his guy and let him know that we had a deal. I was going to pick it up at the drop off point later tonight. It was time to finish another novel that wouldn't have a happy ending. But then again, maybe it is a successful conclusion. If Jackson pulled another stunt by bothering Natalie or me, I had a bullet with his name on it.

Chapter 23

Natalie

I looked out the window into the backyard and saw Marcus and Manny talking. They seemed incredibly close lately, and I had seen Marcus's phone light up more than once with Manny's name on the screen. I found it odd that he would become best buddies with someone who helped to beat his ass. Although, I was happy they weren't trying to kill each other, either.

Most of the guests were gone now. Jessie and his girlfriend were lounging on the couch, watching a movie. Well, Jessie was watching, but ole girl was asleep. I have the hardest time remembering her name. She had several glasses of wine during our celebration and was out like a light. Mr. and Mrs. Colbert left to go home and check on Mia. They offered to send an Uber to get her, but Mia told them she wasn't feeling well and wanted to stay home. I'm assuming she had no idea that Marcus was going to propose when she called me. I'd texted her several times throughout the night to check on her, and each time she responded that she was fine. However, she wasn't fine, and I knew it.

I took Trenton to our bedroom to put him down in his crib for the night and think about how I was going to handle this Jackson situation. As soon as I sat down on the bed, Pepper jumped in my lap. I took off his doggie tux and ran my hand gently through his soft fur. I knew he was feeling a little neglected since Trenton was born, so I scooped him into my arms. He arched his head up and kissed my face while I rubbed his belly. Mr. Powell told me to let him handle it, but it's been two weeks, and he hadn't said anything about what he was going to do to teach him a lesson. I might have to do it myself, but I still had no idea exactly how I would do it, though. The plan had to be flawless with no clues leading back to me.

As I rocked my first baby, Marcus' phone rang. He must have put it on the nightstand to charge. He normally doesn't receive calls this late. I reached over to see who it was in case I needed to take it to him. I immediately recognized the area code and answered.

"Hello," I said.

A startled woman replied, "I think I have the wrong number."

"No, you have the right number. Why are you calling him?"

"Umm, I just wanted to talk. I'm sorry. I won't call again," said Lisa.

"I don't know how you got this number, but I suggest you delete it as soon as you hang up. My fiancé no longer needs to hear from you or any other woman he used to fuck." I had been drinking, and I was ready to let her, Jackson, Chanel, and anybody else have a piece of my mind.

"Fiancé?"

"Yes, Lisa. He proposed to the mother of his child. The woman he lives with. We share a bed and a life, and we are going to get married."

"Well, I guess congratulations are in order," she said in a somber tone.

"Keep them. The only thing I need from you is to remember that I'm his present and his future. You

ma'am, are his past. Don't dial this number again. Have I
made myself clear?"

"Crystal clear, but the only reason I called was because Jackson told me Marcus said he needed to speak to
me. *He* gave me this number."

"Jackson is a pathological liar. Don't believe anything
he tells you, especially as it relates to *my* man. He would
just love to tear up our happy home. I refuse to let him
or anyone else he tries to recruit to help him. There is
nothing here for you, and if Marcus needs to talk, he has
me for that. Goodbye." I hung up, blocked her number,
and deleted the call. When Marcus and I turned over a
new leaf, we gave each other the pass codes to our
phones. I never thought I had a reason to use it. Now,
I'll be checking periodically.

Jackson had some nerve. So, the games have begun.
Well, I have a few tricks of my own. While I was mentally orchestrating my revenge, someone knocked loudly on
the front door. Who in the world would be coming to
our house this late? Maybe someone forgot something.

I put Pepper down, checked on Trenton, and made
my way to the living room. Pepper followed close
behind. I assumed Jessie answered the door. Standing in
our living room were two police officers, and one of
them was in the process of putting handcuffs on my
brother. As I opened my mouth to protest, he said, "It's
okay, Sis. I'm going to go peacefully. I didn't want to
wake up the entire house. The last thing we need is to get
Grammy's pressure up."

It wasn't okay, and I didn't care about waking up
Grammy. "Officers, this is my brother and my home.
Please tell me, what the meaning of this is?"

"Your brother is being arrested for the assault and robbery of a Mr. Marcus Colbert," said one officer with a large gut in a tight uniformed shirt that looked like the buttons were about to pop off. He then began to recite the Miranda rights. "You have the right to remain silent. Anything you say can and will be used against you in a court of law........."

I ran to the back door and screamed, "Marcus! Marcus!" as loudly as I could. Marcus and Manny halted whatever they were talking about and rushed into the house. I looked at him with pleading eyes and said, "Tell them you're not pressing charges. Tell them everything is fine. Don't let them take my brother."

"Officers, I am Marcus Colbert, and this is my soon-to-be brother-in-law. What is this about?" he asked.

The officer continued, "You have the right to an attorney. If you cannot afford one, one will be appointed to you . . ."

The other officer turned toward us and tried to explain. "Mr. Colbert, you were attacked and robbed in a park a few months ago, correct?"

"Yes."

"Well, we received a tip that this man, Jessie Tellis, is responsible and that he would be here tonight."

Manny stepped forward. "Then, you are probably looking for me, as well."

"Why yes, we are, Mr. Thomas. Please turn around and put your hands behind your head."

Manny did as he was told, and the other officer began putting handcuffs on him as well.

"Marcus, do something!" I screamed. Pepper was now aware that I was upset. She bared her teeth and growled in the officers' direction. I picked him up before he tried to be a hero and got us all in trouble.

Marcus took a few steps toward the officers, but the "stand down look" one of them gave caused him to freeze in his tracks. "Officers, there is no need to do this. I know they did it. However, we have worked it out amongst ourselves. I have no desire to press changes," he said.

Eyeing Marcus cautiously, the officer he was nearest to said, "Sir, this is an open investigation. Therefore, when we know who committed the crime, we must arrest them. However, you are welcome to come to his hearing and talk to the judge about dropping the charges. Since today is Friday, it will probably be Monday or Tuesday before they can make bail."

Next week? That was horrible news.

"Officer, my brother has an important shoot this weekend; he was flying out first thing in the morning to film a movie. You have to let him go," I said.

"No shit. Well, I guess you better call Steven Spielberg and let him know he won't make it," said the other officer with a smirk. He had finished reciting the Miranda rights and was trying to maneuver Jessie toward the door.

"Shut up, Natalie *and* Marcus," said Jessie. "You are only making things worse. Let me handle this." He then grunted. The handcuffs were extremely uncomfortable and tight. He was twice as big as the officer, who seemed to be trying to show my brother who the boss was by being unnecessarily rough. Jessie looked at his girlfriend over his shoulder. She was snoring soundly on the couch. "Wake my baby up and tell her what happened. She'll know what to do," he instructed.

Manny had been pretty quiet up until this point, standing calmly by Jessie's side. "Call my dad, Nat Nat. He's retired Nashville PD. He'll take care of everything," he said.

I'm sure he said that for the officers' info, not mine. I knew all about his dad. He was probably hoping that the boys in blue bond would help him in some way, but the news that he was a part of the NPD family got no reaction from the officers. I nodded, then went over to the couch and shook drunken beauty in an effort to wake her. She barely stirred. I started to slap her and then thought better of it. I would have to give her the play-by-play in the morning after she slept off the effects of tonight's celebration. There was very little she could do to help my brother tonight. What were the odds of me being engaged, and my brother being arrested the same night?

The officers escorted Jessie and Manny out the door and down to their squad car while Marcus, Pepper, and I followed. "I'll take care of this," said Marcus.

Jessie responded, "I think you've done enough. Take care of my sister and nephew."

Manny looked at him and said, "Exactly, remember your appointment."

A familiar car was parked across the street. There was Jackson, watching the show, and he didn't even try to hide. He sat there with the window down and grinned at us like a hobo who won the lottery. He noticed me looking and waved. I extended my perfectly manicured middle finger at him.

Marcus saw the exchange, and wasn't pleased. He wrapped his arms around me and kissed me on the cheek. I threw up my left hand with my palm facing me and wriggled it so that he could see the blinding rock on my hand. This probably wasn't the best time to demonstrate our dedication, but we both wanted him to know our love was solid despite his attempts to infiltrate it. Jackson's smile disappeared.

"I think I need to have a few words with him. I bet I know where that 'tip' came from," said Marcus. He released me and began walking toward the car. I didn't try to stop him. Jackson scowled and quickly sped off.

That spawn of Satan had made good on his promise to try to ruin everyone I loved.

Marcus came back, looked at me and said, "I have something to do. I'll be back."

Where was he going this time of night?

Chapter 24

Marcus

Calm down, Marcus, is what I kept saying to myself. The smug look on Jackson's face as the cops hauled off Jessie and Manny kept flashing in my mind. I felt like the fictional boxer Rocky Balboa prepping to battle Drago. Better yet, I would say that I was a hand working to scratch an irritating itch.

I kept my appointment and picked up my piece. It was in my lap, fully loaded, and ready to go to work. I raised my cup to my lips only for nothing to meet my mouth in return; I was out of coffee. My hands had a subtle quiver as I turned off my headlights and sank down in the driver's seat. The beeping, due to the keys still being in the ignition, began to bother me, so I removed them, and soon the radio would fade off as well. I was able to smell nature through the crack in the window that allowed the cloud of smoke that fell from my mouth to exit the vehicle. I remembered what I promised Natalie in regards to giving up smoking, but I didn't care. I needed this cigarette to calm my nerves. The clouds were still blanketed by darkness when I pulled up. It was a little past four in the morning. I was surprised at how alive the city still was at this time of night, or morning, depending on how you looked at it. Who would have thought that a village of vampires surrounded me? Then I thought about how alive we were when we were younger; Jackson and I, the two of us . . . my ace, my brother. The thought of it all still baffled me. How was he able to treat me like this?

I hid my face as a car slowly passed by and turned into a nearby driveway. The woman inside was breaking her neck, trying to identify the man behind the wheel of my vehicle. I guess I appeared to be an intruder in the night, and she was right. I knew it would be no time before she called the cops. I reached for my keys and started the ignition; it was time to change locations.

When I pulled up closer to Jackson's place, I parked a good twenty yards away by a curb that had been spray painted with the latest teenage lingo. My phone kept lighting up. It was from Natalie. When I left the house, she kept telling me not to do anything stupid. I guess I'm not too good of a listener these days.

I still had the shakes; my body felt like I had eaten the coffee or snorted it through my nostrils, going straight into my bloodstream. The effect was strong, or it was just my anxiety kicking in. Either way, I was a nervous wreck.

I ducked down in my seat. Being a predator was hard work, and I was terrible at it. Natalie didn't have to worry about me taking on this type of work full time. I had no plan. I had no gloves. No alibi—nothing. It was just my ego, me, and my piece.

Beads of sweat began to form on my forehead. My face grew hot, and my stomach began to churn. Coffee always did this to me. It wasn't a good time to have the bubble guts. I was highly uncomfortable. I turned on the air conditioner, hoping the temperature change would settle my mood and stomach. That's when I realized that my headlights were still on. Shit. I heard some dogs barking loudly. Shit. I saw a light come on and someone peeping through their blinds, followed by their lights going out. I was spotted; I had to move, again.

When I turned on the ignition, I saw some blue and white lights flashing in my rearview. They were coming full speed ahead. My heart accelerated, and my tongue couldn't keep up with my head. Too many thoughts raced through it. What would I say? What reason could I give? I had a gun on me. I panicked. As I was about to speed off, the police car zoomed past me, and I was relieved. "Thank God," I said to myself. Then I thought, *Should I be thanking God for not getting caught for a crime I was about to commit?* Well, at least, it sounded good.

I pulled off slowly and checked my surroundings. The person was still staring through the blinds. More lights came on and then off in the neighborhood. *This must be a neighborhood watch thing*, I thought. I decided to go around the block and wait things out for a good thirty minutes. I checked the time, and it was approaching five. I knew Jackson would be getting ready to head to the gym in an hour. The timing was working out perfectly. All this time, I kept hearing the sound of sirens.

I decided to go to the nearest gas station to get more coffee and to relieve myself in the restroom. I put my gun under the seat. As I exited, I was no longer nervous. I had made my mind up that it was time. No turning back now. This was for my sanity, my family, and me. I hoped that God would forgive me for what I was about to do.

***

Have you ever heard the saying, if you want to make God laugh, then tell him your plans? Well, he must have been on a cloud laughing, because the plan I had in my head just didn't pan out the way I anticipated. When I was at the gas station waiting in line to purchase my cup of coffee and gum, I saw my therapist, Dr. Ward. I must admit, it was weird seeing her outside of her work attire. She was wearing some black leggings and sneakers. She had her hair tied to the back in a ponytail. Her skin glowed a bronze radiance. She must have been headed to or coming from the gym.

"Fancy meeting you here," she said.

I smiled. "Indeed."

"I assume things are going well for you?"

I nodded my head.

A delivery truck driver wedged his large body between our private space en route to the cake snack stand. No "excuse me," or variation of it escaped his lips. Before I could address it, she waved me off.

"Not worth it," she said.

She was right. "Early morning or late night?" I asked.

She laughed. "I can't tell the difference sometimes."

I always thought she was beautiful. Perfect teeth and toned from head to toe, full lips, positive energy, and I wondered how her husband let her get away. I glanced at my watch.

"Got somewhere to be?" she asked.

"No, not in particular. Why do you ask?"

"You've checked your watch like four times since we started talking."

I chuckled nervously. "Didn't notice," I replied. I would be a horrible criminal. I know I had *he's up to something* written across my forehead.

"Are you sure things are okay?" she probed.

"I assure you . . . things are well," I said in my best attempt to sound confident. Then I continued, "I officially proposed to Natalie. I had a ring and got down on one knee this time."

Her eyes lit up. I knew this would take her mind off me and stop her questioning. "Wow! I guess congratulations are in order then, Mr. Colbert." She playfully nudged me on the shoulder.

"I guess so," I responded.

I was next up to be checked out. I placed my cup of coffee on the counter. Then, the thought hit me. There was no way I could do what I set out to do because someone was able to identify me and place me near the scene of the would-be crime. God was either protecting that fool Jackson or me. Running into Dr. Ward prevents me from furthering my elaborate plan that was not well thought out anyway. Now, I needed to get back to the drawing board to devise a better plan.

Before Dr. Ward and I said our goodbyes, she invited me for another session to discuss where I was in my healing process. I agreed to set up an appointment soon. I exited the store and sat in the gas station parking lot for what seemed like an eternity. I took slow and subtle sips of my coffee in between pulls of my cigarette. The damn ashes were everywhere inside the car. It would have to be cleaned.

Sometimes you don't have to set a trap to catch a rat. You can just follow its trail of droppings to the place it dwells. Hate is like a rat in that way. I would be lying if I said that Jackson and his actions didn't blindside me. At first, it was the hurt and betrayal of a loved one that ignited my anger. Then, I understood that Jackson had never been a true friend to me. There I was sitting in the parking lot at the point of no return. It was time to return the hate that was given. Damn a plan.

***

I circled the block a couple of times to check the temperature of the neighbors before proceeding to the area where Jackson lived. I guess the nosy neighbors were now at ease as it was eerily quiet. The sun was beginning to rise, and I saw some joggers wave a hand or two as I drove by. Even the darkness seemed to be against me. I couldn't hide in daylight.

There would be no retribution from me that day. I thought, *Maybe I could throw a brick or something through his windshield. Naw, that would be a move a scorned woman would make.* I laughed to myself because now I was angry and a sexist. I shook my head and decided to circle the block again, and this time, just drive by Jackson's house.

The light from my phone wouldn't stop. It was Natalie for like the thousandth time. I turned the phone over on its face as I eased onto Jackson's street—and then suddenly stopped. Luckily, I wasn't accelerating too much, or the sound of the rubber against the road would have been loud and brought me some unwanted attention. I squinted my eyes to make sure they weren't lying to me.

In front of Jackson's house was a trail of police cars and an ambulance. I drove past as my rubbernecking ambition got the best of me. I panicked as I saw a stretcher being wheeled out of the front door with a white sheet over a body. A couple of people were standing in his yard with their hands over their mouths. Some were crying while others looked like they were trying to make sense of it all. One lady, who had a short blond cut atop her head, was holding a leash to a dog that was running amuck, and talking to an officer as his hand was working his pad.

As I passed Jackson's house, a mixed feeling of emotions began to overwhelm me. I laughed and cried all at the same damn time. I turned the phone back over and noticed that I had eighteen missed calls, twenty-five texts, and thirteen Instagram messages from Natalie. I wanted to call, but I decided to wait to discuss what I had seen with her. Damn. I wanted to get out and check to see who was under that sheet, but my heart already knew who it was. Jackson was dead. Someone had already beat me to the punch. I headed home.

Once I pulled into my garage, I stepped out of the car, walked toward the trunk, and looked toward the sky. *God, I'm not even going to ask you about all of this because, honestly, I don't need to or want to know.* I ran my hand over my face, shook my head, and walked inside my home to tell Natalie the news.

Chapter 25

Natalie

It's odd how the death of one man sent a calming wind over the lives of multiple people. Usually, death disrupts and causes great pain and grief, but when we received the news of Jackson's death, there seemed to be a collective sigh of relief from both of us, my family members, friends, and business acquaintances. We were all shocked when we learned that Jackson had been murdered, but we were even more shocked at the brutality of the act. He was shot two times in the chest and once in the face according to the coroner's report. Then, he was left to die a slow, agonizing death as the life seeped out of his body. No one seems to know who did it. The police had a list of persons of interest. I had my own list as well.

Originally, I thought Marcus might have done it since he was gone for several hours and would not answer his phone the night it occurred. He admitted to me that he was sitting outside of Jackson's home but never even worked up the nerve to knock on the door. I know my man well enough to know if he had done it, he would have told me. Jessie and Manny couldn't have done it because they were both in jail, thanks to Jackson. That still left any number of those women Jackson took sexual footage of and blackmailed. Hell, even I wanted to kill him for what he tried to do to Mia and me. But when he was a friend, he was a good friend, even if he did have ulterior motives of trying to tear my family apart so he could have me for himself. However, I'm not exactly mourning his death, and I am happy that he is no longer able to terrorize people at will. That sick, spoiled bastard wreaked havoc on people's lives just because they didn't do what he wanted them to do. Talk about a control freak.

His death actually took a huge stress off Marcus and me. We were no longer concerned that he'd tell lies and ruin our careers and reputations. Even Jessie and Manny were better off. After Jackson was murdered, the charges against them were mysteriously dropped, and they were released from jail the same morning. Those two came to my house and demanded that I cook them breakfast before they left. I was told it was the least I could do for their troubles. I'm so happy they were able to get past the altercation with Marcus. I need the three most important men in my life to get along.

For some, Jackson's antics left scars. Mia shared with me that ever since he attacked her, she can't get the scent of him out of her nostrils, and occasionally, he comes to her in her dreams. He doesn't say anything; he just stares at her and licks his lips, and I know that look. He did it the night he lured me to that hotel room. That sinister, lustful look sent chills down my spine, and I'm a grown woman. I can only imagine what it does to a teenager. On the nights she stays with us, I hold her in my arms and let her know everything is going to be all right. As long as Marcus and I have breath in our bodies, nobody is ever going to hurt her again.

Mia and I both decided not to tell Marcus that Jackson attacked her. We're afraid he would try to shoot up the casket at his funeral. Maybe one day, years from now, we'll tell him, but for now, it's better that he doesn't know. I'm not sure how Marcus feels about Jackson's death. He seems sad, yet angry. I tried to get him to talk about it, but he won't.

I asked my boss, Mr. Powell, if he knew anything about Jackson's death. He laughed and then disavowed any knowledge of foul play. All he said was, "I'm glad he's dead. Whoever did it did the world a favor."

The only people who don't seem relieved about Jackson's death are his parents. As Mr. and Mrs. Smith's only child and heir to their company's legacy, they now have to find a new successor. Mr. Smith had been grooming Jackson for the role from birth. Gone are their dreams for grandchildren and any other plans they had for the son they adored. Jackson's death may be one mystery that never gets solved.

Today is the funeral, and Marcus and I decided to go. We were all the best of friends once, and Jackson was an intricate part of our lives. When times were good, they were really good. I guess we're going to say goodbye to the memory of Jackson and not the reality. We also want to give our respects to the old man. Jackson's father was kind to me until I violated company policy by dating a client, which I have no regrets over whatsoever. That client turned out to be the love of my life, the father of my child, and will soon be my husband. It was a hard, long road that got us here, but we are in a beautiful place together, and I can't wait to walk down the aisle, meet him at the altar, and officially become Mrs. Marcus Colbert. The good news is that I only have to wait until tomorrow! We decided just to do it, and in less than 24 hours, we will be joined in holy matrimony during a very intimate ceremony at his parents' home. I picked out the most gorgeous dress I've ever seen. I even found the cutest baby tux for Trenton. We plan to have a reception in a few months to celebrate with our extended friends and family, but for now, all I need to do is to get married with Trenton and our immediate families present.

I decided that I wanted to straighten my coily hair for the funeral and the wedding. My flat irons are broken, but Grammy volunteered to press it for me. She hasn't pressed my hair since I was fifteen. I'm hoping her hands are a little gentler in her older age than they were back then. I walked into the kitchen and sat in a chair while she heated the pressing comb on one of the eyes of the stove. Trenton sat nearby in his bouncer. He had eaten his breakfast and was dozing off to sleep. Every time I look at my sweet boy, my heart swells with emotion. He is definitely the best thing that's ever happened to me. He's teething and has been a bit fussy lately. If we're lucky, he'll stay asleep until Grammy is done with my hair.

"Where's your grease?" she asked. "I got some if you need it."

"Grammy, nobody uses grease anymore. Just run the comb through my hair," I said.

"What? No grease? Y'all children done lost your minds, but I'll do as you ask."

She began to undo one of the four large plaits I put my hair in last night after I washed it. Once she finished, she then took a large wide-toothed comb and combed through my tresses.

"I forgot how thick your hair is. This might take awhile." She took a deep breath and then tested the pressing comb to see if it was hot enough.

That was the last thing I wanted to hear. "I have two hours before I have to get up and get dressed," I said.

"And I'll probably need the whole two. You got hair just like your mother had. By the time she was ten, I was sending her to the beauty shop because I didn't have all day to be pressing no hair. Your granddaddy and I had a business to run." She put the comb back down on the stove. "Baby, I can't press no dry hair." She then reached into the pocket of her housedress and pulled out a jar of green Ultra Sheen hair grease. Then she opened up the jar, scooped out a little, and began rubbing it on my hair. I decided to let her do it rather than object. The sooner we get this over with, the better.

Grammy began humming softly as she worked. Then, she broke out in song. "Jesus is on the main line, tell him what chu waaaaant. Ooooh, Jesus is on the main line. Tell'em what chu waaaant. You just call him up and tell'em what chu waaaaant." She paused for a moment before she parted my hair and went to work on the next section. "Baby, I think I'm going to leave the day after the wedding. So, you and Marcus need to find you a new babysitter. I know he'll be returning to work soon."

"But Grammy, why? I thought you liked being here. You and Marcus are even getting along."

She chuckled. "I do, but you two need your space. I'm starting to miss having my own space, too. Also, it's not that I disliked Marcus. I disliked what he was doing to you. That was why I had him shot."

I jerked my head. "Stop playing, Grammy! You know you didn't shoot nobody."

"Stop moving before I burn you. Of course, I didn't shoot him. I had him shot."

This time, I jumped and got burned by that 200-degree hot comb.

"Sit still girl, and listen, or I'll burn you again. Do you remember your granddaddy?"

"Papa Chase? Of course, I do."

"Did you know he was in a gang?"

I started to jerk my head around again, but I didn't want to get burned. Showing up to the wedding with scars on me wouldn't be cute. I stayed facing forward and said, "Grammy, no he wasn't. Are you getting dementia?"

"No, I don't have the D-word. I got more sense than you do. Your papa was in a gang, but he wasn't nobody's street thug on account that he was a businessman. He was one of the higher-ups, and he didn't take no part in illegal activity himself, but he did help call the shots and hide the money that was generated from illegal activity. He also gave counsel when asked. When he died, I sold our store to the gang. As his widow, I am afforded certain protections and perks. When I heard about all the problems you were having, I came to see for myself. You always were kind of on the weak side. There was no way I was gonna stand by and watch some boy in a man's body run over my only granddaughter. So, I called in a favor. Now, I didn't tell them to kill him, so don't think that. They were only supposed to scare him, but when you send killers to do a job, you get what you get."

I sat quietly while she spoke. I was going to hear this entire joke out. I knew the punch line was going to be hilarious.

"Because of him, my Jessie and his friend were turning to violence, trying to defend your honor. You were round here pregnant and losing your mind while he was gallivanting around with that bald-headed girl like he was Mr. Big Stuff or something. He needed to be taken down a peg or two, and I'm just the somebody to do it. Yep, gangs are actually quite well connected. There are doctors like obstetricians, who administer medication to pregnant women, in gangs. There are police officers, lawyers, and judges in gangs. Yep, any occupation you can think of, there is a gang member in it or someone willing to strike enough fear into someone to get what you need to be done, for a price. But you better believe that there are killers who can take someone out, and no one has any idea who did it."

I was finally putting two together. Marcus' shooting, Chanel's miscarriage, and Jackson's death were all connected. I sat as stiff as a board while she continued to do my hair and talk as if taking hits out on people was the most natural thing in the world.

"Grammy, why would you do that?" I softly asked.

"Because NOBODY messes with my kinfolk! Where I'm from, you handle your enemies in silence. You don't get all on social media making threats and telling the world your next move. You just make it and let the outcome be what it is. That's why I took on the burden and didn't tell you in case things got all screwed up. I'd say they turned out pretty well. Everybody is good now, and they are free to live their lives the way they see fit. I'm telling you this so you can get your shit together, young lady. I expect you to make wiser decisions in your life from here on out. I've got enough blood on my hands. I set things up nicely for you, your fella, and this baby. Take my gift and use it wisely. He's learned his lesson. You better be good to him, and he'll be good to you. Cook him some good food, give him some good loving, and don't be nagging him. Give him a couple more babies to occupy his time," she chuckled. "Y'all gone be juuuust fine. Well, now, you know. I know you ain't stupid enough to tell anyone. Don't you tell a soul!

You hear me, girl?"

"Yes, ma'am," I said softly. This wasn't a joke. There would be no punch line and no hearty laugh at the end.

"When you go to your room you are going to find an envelope in your fancy drawers' drawer. That is my wedding present to you and Marcus. Do whatever you like with it," said Grammy.

I was dumbfounded and too scared to move. My grammy was hell, fire, and brimstone in a sheer floral housedress. I sat there in silence while she did my hair. Grammy hummed the entire time like she hadn't orchestrated the murders of a man and an unborn child and the attempted murder of my Marcus. I loved this old woman, but she was crazy. I know Marcus and I promised each other no more secrets, but Jackson attacking Mia and this one couldn't be helped. When she finished, I hugged her and inhaled her perfume like I used to do as a child. She still wore Red Door. I tried not to shake too much, but I was clearly rattled. She laughed.

"You are welcome, baby. Go look at your hair. I know that was a lot to take in, but you'll be all right. Now, go get ready for that fune. I'm going to go pack my things."

Before I went to the bathroom in my bedroom to peep her handiwork, I opened my lingerie drawer. I didn't immediately see anything, but then I noticed a manila envelope under one of my black silk nightgowns. I opened it and inside were two large stacks of hundred-dollar bills. There had to be at least $30,000 in it. I started to ask Grammy where she got that kind of money from, but then I changed my mind. It was probably better if I didn't know, and I needed to get dressed. Marcus would be back from washing our cars soon, and it wouldn't take him any time at all to get ready. He hates being late.

Grammy was right about one thing. It was time for her to go home.

Chapter 26

Marcus

How did we get from there to here? This is something I kept asking myself over the last 24 hours. Then as I marveled at my mother and father, sitting, fingers locked together, I asked myself, how can we get from here to there?

As I think about the maturation process of Natalie and my relationship, one word comes to mind—consistency. This is something that I've long struggled with. From my relationships and commitments to the women in my life to my inconsistent clarity of myself, I've struggled to find the constant balance in it all. Maybe life is not meant to have such consistency. However, I know that for us to get to where my father and mother are in life, I—we—need to find that level of consistency for the sake of our little guy Trenton.

These past 24 hours, or this past year, for that matter, hasn't reflected the consistency I'm striving for. But now as I think about it some more, maybe there has been some level of consistency. It was my keen ability to find a way to fuck something up. Looking back on when I first learned that Natalie was pregnant with Trenton and I wasn't fully over losing Lisa. Then, me getting involved with Chanel soon afterward, the confrontation with Jessie and Manny, Jackson's betrayal, and my being shot, Trenton being born, Chanel's miscarriage and more betrayal by Jackson, me burying a once near and dear friend. All of this happened in a short span, but here I am, Marcus J. Colbert, and I'm about to marry the one constant throughout it all—Natalie.

As I watched her walk down the aisle, with Jessie escorting her, in that dress that accentuated all her curves, it made me tear up. I'm glad he could take a quick break from filming to come. We didn't have a large audience, just close family. I no longer associate with friends. We're either family, or we're not. There will be no more in-between.

Natalie had a glow about her as she approached me. Our eyes met and locked. Both of us were misty-eyed. I extended my hand to catch hers, and we locked fingers. She was close enough for me to get a whiff of her sweet cinnamon breath. We continued to gaze into each other's eyes, each trying to read the mind of the other. Love is present, and our minds can reflect on the journey, but our eyes are on the destination.

I looked out into the small gathering of family. My sister, Mia, holding Trenton. Our eyes caught. We smiled. She has been distant with me as of late, but most teenagers push away from their "elders" at some point in their lives in hopes of finding their own independence. I just pray that she doesn't follow my steps but instead, learn from them.

I see Grammy, working her gum with her dentures. That lady is one mean bat, but she's my Grammy now. She stared me down and patted her purse three times. I don't know what that meant, so I just nod my head and smile.

Mannie is sitting with his lady and kids. One of them clearly doesn't appreciate having to wear a suit and keeps tugging on the collar.

My mother and father nodded at me as a sign of approval.

I stared into Natalie's eyes, took her hand, and placed it on top of mine. I want more children with her, and I promised myself those pregnancies would be drama free. She is the only woman in my life and the only woman that will carry my children.

The pastor said all of the tradition hoopla. We said our vows. Then, the part I was waiting for, like a child at Christmas arrived. He pronounced us man and wife. The love of my life, my friend, and my amazing lover is now my wife.

We kissed—a long, wet one. I heard people whistling, cheering, and clapping. Natalie cried. We kissed again, and she cried some more. We turned to look out at our family, and I asked myself, *where do we go from here?* We are in a much better place than where we were before. Blessings. Wherever it is, I know it will be full of blessings.

Stay Connected

You can follow the Where Do We Go From Here series at Facebook.com/jmwheredowegofromhere.

Jae

www.jaehendersonauthor.com

Mario D. King

www.mariodking.com

About the Authors

Jae Henderson

Jae Henderson's writing exists to motivate others. She invites readers to join her on a most entertaining journey that imparts some sage wisdom and assists readers in further realizing that we may not be perfect, but we serve a perfect God. Now the author of five books, she began in 2011 with her debut inspirational romance novel, Someday. In 2012, she released the sequel, Someday, Too, and followed it with the finale to her trilogy, Forever and a Day in 2013. She followed those with two books of inspirational short stories, Things Every Good Woman Should Know, Volume 1 and 2.

Jae is a graduate of the University of Memphis where she earned a BA in communications and an MA in English. She is the former host and producer of On Point, a once popular talk show geared toward youth and young adults. Other accomplishments have included serving as a contributing writer for the award-winning, syndicated Tom Joyner Morning Show and a successful career as a voice-over artist. Her signature voice has been heard in hundreds of commercials and even a couple of cartoons. When Jae isn't writing, she works as a public relations specialist. She currently resides in her hometown of Memphis, Tennessee.

Mario D. King

Mario D. King writes to change the world with works that will spark an educational revolution. He made his literary debut in 2013 with the release of his hip-hop novella, *The Crisis Before Midlife*. Met with rave reviews by readers, he decided to continue to encourage change in the community through literature with the release of his first nonfiction project, *What's Happening Brother: How to strategize in a system designed for you to fail*. In it, Mario provides a realistic discourse that embraces accountability and responsibility to systematically address the problems ailing the black community. Through his meticulous research, he explores solutions in education, entrepreneurship, leadership, community, and spirituality, amongst several other topics, to transform the thinking of black men and their respective counterparts. His love for the black family propelled him to embark on a different kind of journey with *Where Do We Go from Here?* King hopes that by helping to illustrate how misguided relationships can negatively affect the lives of all involved, people will make wiser decisions and strengthen black families. Be sure to check out his latest release, *Low Reign*.

Mario received his bachelor's degree in communications from the University of Tennessee at Chattanooga where he studied global culture and communication, psychology and sociology. He received his MBA from Kaplan University and will continue to stir up change and motivate those with whom he comes in contact. A native of Memphis, Tennessee, this husband and father of three now lives in Charlotte, North Carolina, where he continues to be a positive influence in his community.

Made in the USA
Columbia, SC
03 June 2024